JADE CHARLOTTE

Power Play

Contents

Title Page

Power Play

A Forbidden Hockey Romance

Book One of the Off-The-Ice Series
by Jade Charlotte

Content Warnings

This novel contains mature and potentially triggering content, including:

- **Age-gap relationship**
- **Power imbalance** (Boss/Employee dynamic)
- **Forbidden romance** (Father/son's ex-girlfriend trope)
- **Emotional manipulation** (past and present)
- **Cheating / Infidelity themes**
- **Parental abandonment / estranged parent**
- **Grief and unresolved family trauma**
- **Explicit sexual content** (consensual but rough, including light choking and dominance/submission themes)
- **Strong language and adult themes throughout**

Please note: While the romance is consensual and emotionally complex, the relationships depicted are messy, morally grey, and may not be comfortable for all readers.

Dedication

For the ones who pretend they want soft love—
but secretly crave the kind that bruises.
For those who want to be ruined,
not just touched.

This book is for you.
And you know exactly why.

1

Chapter 1

Lexi

I should've seen it coming. The late-night texts angled just out of sight. The sudden need for "space" after every bad game. The way he stopped looking at me like I was his girl and started looking through me like I was a recurring task he'd already rescheduled a dozen times.

Still, nothing—and I mean nothing—could've prepped me for the Olympic-level gut-punch of walking into Ethan Wilson's apartment—our apartment in all but paperwork—and finding him in full slime ball form.

With two girls.

In his jersey.

One of them giggled like this was a scene from some trashy reality show and not, you know, the implosion of my actual life. The scent of cheap perfume and betrayal clung to the air, clawing at my senses.

My legs stopped working. I just stood there in the doorway, heart thudding like a kick drum in my chest. My brain lagged like a frozen app. I'd worn lip gloss for him. I'd picked up his favourite takeout. I'd come here to try.

And this? This is what I walked into?

For a second, I thought I was going to collapse. Then I thought I might throw up. Then I wondered if it was possible to do both at once and still walk away with any dignity.

Instead, I stayed standing. My arms folded across my chest, tight like a shield, while rage started simmering under my skin like a pot just seconds from boiling over.

"Are you serious"

My voice came out weirdly calm, considering the nuclear fallout happening behind my ribs. That calm scared me more than if I'd screamed.

Ethan blinked at me like I was the intruder. His shirt was halfway off. Hair already messy from—nope. We're not finishing that mental image. He had the audacity to sigh.

"Lexi—"

"No. Don't you 'Lexi' me," I snapped, raising a hand like a stop sign made of fury. "This what you've been doing during all those 'early nights'? Resting up for your next betrayal?"

One of the girls—not looking, still refusing to acknowledge her as anything other than a bad decision in lip liner—cleared her throat. "Maybe I should go—"

"Wow. Incredible idea," I said, eyes never leaving Ethan's face. "You should definitely go. Maybe both of you. Get out while he's still got a mattress that hasn't seen a felony."

Ethan looked annoyed. Not ashamed. Not sorry. Just... inconvenienced. Like I'd walked in on him doing laundry instead of cheating.

Typical.

"We need to talk," he said, like this was a misunderstanding.

2

Like I hadn't just caught him red-handed in a Jersey Shore remake.

I laughed. Dry, sharp. The kind of laugh that cut my throat on the way out. "No, you need to shut the hell up. We're done. Game over. Season canceled. Delete your roster."

I turned on my heel like my spine was made of steel and not heartbreak and caffeine. I didn't slam the door—I closed it. Deliberate. Controlled. Way more power in that.

The cold night air hit me like a slap, and I just stood there on the sidewalk, keys still in hand, shaking.

I couldn't stop seeing it. Him. Them. That jersey.

My stomach twisted. My eyes stung. I didn't cry—but I could feel the tears lurking, waiting for a moment of weakness.

And still—under all of it, buried beneath the betrayal and fury and that deep, aching humiliation—was something else.

Relief.

Because I didn't have to wonder anymore. I didn't have to defend him. I didn't have to beg him to choose me.

He already had.

And not choosing me? That was the clearest choice of all.

For the first time in two years, I felt free.

Even if it hurt like hell.

I didn't think. I just moved.

I shoved my phone into my bag and started walking. Fast. No plan, no direction—just the need to *not be there* anymore. Every step was a frantic, breathless attempt to outrun the image burned into my brain.

Rachel's place wasn't far. Five blocks, give or take. I didn't remember the walk. I just remember her door opening, warm light spilling out, and her face crumpling when she saw mine.

She didn't ask anything.

She just pulled me in and let me fall apart.

I don't even know what I said—maybe nothing. Maybe everything. I just know I ended up curled on her couch, knees to my chest, wrapped in one of her oversized hoodies while she pressed a mug of tea into my shaking hands like it could fix something.

"You're moving in," she said simply, like it wasn't even up for discussion. "Spare room's yours. It's closer to your work anyway."

I blinked at her, raw and ragged. "You serious?"

She nodded. "You think I'm gonna let you got back to that spineless asshole?"

And just like that, I started crying.

Not the pretty kind. Not the soft movie kind. The real, ugly, gasping kind that feels like ripping grief out by the roots.

She just held me tighter.

My whole world had cracked open, but Rachel was the glue. She always had been.

* * *

A week later, we moved everything out while Ethan was out of town.

Rachel showed up with coffee, sunglasses, and the kind of get-shit-done energy that could level a small country. We didn't speak much. We didn't need to.

I packed faster than I expected—like if I slowed down, the grief might catch up. Room by room, we erased me from that space. My clothes. My books. The photo on the fridge that used to mean something and now just looked stupid.

4

By the time we finished, the sun was going down. My body ached. My heart felt like it had been used as a punching bag for a week straight. I stood in the now-bare bedroom, staring at the dent in the carpet where my dresser used to be, and suddenly it hit me:

He hadn't called.

Not once.

Not a text. Not a missed call. Not even a pathetic "sorry" to pretend like this hadn't just imploded both our lives.

"He really didn't care," I said, voice barely above a whisper.

Rachel stood beside me, arms crossed, eyes sharp. "No. He just didn't care enough."

That was worse.

I swallowed the lump in my throat and looked around one last time. I wasn't sad it was over.

I was sad it hadn't meant more to him.

Then I walked out and didn't look back.

* * *

FLASHBACK – 1 YEAR AGO

We met on my first day with the team.

I was the new social media manager—nervous, overcaffeinated, and dressed like I was interviewing for Vogue when really I was just trying to make it through my first day without spilling coffee on a player. And he was Ethan Wilson: center for the team, PR disaster, golden boy with a bad reputation and a smirk that should've come with a warning label.

I'd been warned about him. "Stay professional," they said. "Don't get too close," they said. "He's... Ethan."

He lived up to the hype in every way. Cocky, charming, effortlessly hot in that "I don't care and it only makes me hotter" way. But he never crossed a line. At first.

The first few months were... magic. Movie-montage level. He'd stop by my office under the guise of checking out what I was posting on the team account but would always linger too long. He'd bring me coffee—always right, always with a note that made me blush.

He sent me playlists at midnight. Made jokes no one else would dare. He'd brush his fingers against mine like it didn't mean anything, but his eyes would burn like it meant everything.

I still remember the first time he kissed me. Late night. Empty hallway outside the locker room. He looked at me like he was about to ruin something, and I let him.

He kissed me like he'd been waiting his whole life to.

And for a while, it felt like he had.

But somewhere along the way, something shifted.

The texts came slower. His voice got colder. He stopped waiting for me after games. He'd disappear into bars, headlines, and excuses. And when I reached out, I was always too early or too late.

We tried. I tried. We fought, and he said it was stress, pressure, the season. But he never reached for me like he used to. Never looked at me like I was something he wanted to keep.

2

Chapter 2

Lexi

7 Weeks later

There should be a warning label for heartbreak.

Caution: May cause spontaneous crying in grocery store aisles, erratic hair decisions, and severe attachment to rom-coms featuring emotionally stunted men.

It had been seven weeks since 'The Incident'—walking in on Ethan, my now very ex-boyfriend. And while I hadn't exactly bounced back, I had graduated from full-blown sobbing to only slightly soul-crushed with a side of sarcasm.

Tonight was supposed to be my triumphant return to society. Or, at the very least, the first night I left the apartment without looking like a depressed college student in finals week. Rachel had threatened to stage an intervention if I didn't put on real pants.

I pulled the straps of my black backless dress into place, eyeing myself in the mirror with the kind of scrutiny reserved for FBI crime scenes. The dress hugged all the right places and none of the wrong ones, a statement piece in a language I hadn't spoken in weeks: *I still exist, and I might be a problem.*

My hair was loosely curled, my lipstick was fierce, and my heels were tall enough to cause property damage. Rachel had called them my "revenge shoes." She wasn't wrong.

"You're wearing black. That's progress," she said from the doorway, twirling a strand of her red hair, which she'd pulled into a high ponytail that screamed *confident, unbothered, and probably capable of murder.* Her dress was short, red, and glittery, and she looked like she had walked straight out of a music video titled *Unbothered Badass Volume III.*

"Black is versatile," I muttered. "Could be for a funeral. Could be for a party. Who's to say."

Rachel snorted. "Funeral for your tragic taste in men, maybe. Now let's go."

The bar she dragged me to was the kind of place with overpriced drinks, thumping bass, and lighting so dim you could pretend your life wasn't a flaming dumpster. I hated it immediately.

We claimed a booth near the back, sliding into the cracked leather seats with drinks in hand. The bass thumped in our chests like we were sitting inside a heartbeat. While I clung to my drink like it was emotional life support, Rachel scanned the room like a horny hawk on a mission. Just as I was debating whether I could sneak out unnoticed, Maya appeared at the table. She and I worked together—one of those accidental coworker friendships that somehow morphed into real life. Somewhere between shared deadlines and after-work drinks, Rachel, Maya, and I had become an unlikely little trio. Roommates, colleagues, and now besties with benefits— benefits being group chats full of memes and mutual emotional damage.

"Well, if it isn't my two favourite heartbreak disasters," she said, plopping down next to Rachel.

Rachel grinned. "Speak of the devil. Maya, this is the new Lexi 2.0: sassier, single, and about to make some very interesting decisions."

Maya gave me a once-over and a nod of approval. "The dress is giving. The shoes are threatening. I respect the vibe."

"Thanks," I said, smiling despite myself. "I'm trying the 'don't cry, just look hot' method of healing."

"Works every time," Maya said, raising her glass. "Now let's get this party mildly unhinged."

"So," Rachel said, raising her eyebrows in that way that meant she was about to ruin my life. "Are we finally admitting that Ethan was human trash, or do you need another week of tragic playlist curating?""

I groaned. "I just got dumped and emotionally annihilated. A little sympathy wouldn't kill you."

"I *have* sympathy," she said, sipping something neon and dangerous. "But I also have an overwhelming urge to drag you out of this spiral before you start embroidering pillows with his name and setting them on fire."

"Too late," I said, burying my face in my hands. "I started a burn book. Chapter One: Ethan Wilson is a walking warning label."

Rachel let out a delighted laugh. "Okay, fine. But now that we've burned that bridge, what's the plan? Revenge body? Strategic rebound? Blocking him on every platform and pretending he died in a tragic boat explosion?"

"That last one has potential."

She beamed. "Look, I know you've spent the last seven weeks in emotional hibernation—"

"Sweatpants are a lifestyle."

"—but it's time. You need to get out. You need to remember that you're Lexi freaking Michelson."

I sighed. The worst part? She wasn't wrong.

"Fine," I said. "One drink."

Rachel grinned like she'd won a court case. "Please. We both know it's never just one."

And, honestly? She was probably right.

I was halfway through drink number two—still pretending to enjoy the music and not internally spiraling—when I saw him.

Tall. Broad shoulders. That expensive, complicated kind of hot. The kind of man who didn't just walk into a bar— he *commanded* it. He leaned against the bar like it owed him money, his whiskey glass catching the light just right, like the whole room had been designed to spotlight his jawline.

I blinked. Did a double take.

I didn't know him—but I felt like I *should.* Or maybe I just wanted to.

There was something about him. Something... electric. Like danger and charm had gone halfsies on a very expensive suit.

Rachel followed my gaze. Her eyes widened. "Lexi. He's either a hedge fund villain or a tragic love story in the making."

"Maybe both," I muttered, my heart already doing Olympic flips.

Because even though I had no idea who he was, one look told me one very important thing:

I was in trouble.

3

Chapter 3

Lexi

I didn't mean to go to the bar alone. It just sort of happened. Rachel and Maya were deep in conversation, heads bent together, probably conspiring to ruin my love life in a new and exciting way.

I slipped away with my empty glass, weaving through the crowd like someone on a mission. Mostly to refill my drink, partly to cool down from the sudden, inexplicable heat crawling up my neck.

And, okay—*maybe* I wanted another look at him.

He was still there. Same spot. Still leaned against the bar like he owned it.

Which, okay—maybe he did. He looked like the kind of man who casually owned things. Buildings. Companies. Souls.

His eyes flicked toward me the second I stepped up beside him.

I ignored the way my stomach flipped. It was just the vodka. And the heels. And the fact that he was objectively... alarmingly hot.

The bartender barely glanced at me. Too busy pouring top-shelf whiskey into the man's glass.

"I think you skipped me," I said to no one in particular, trying for nonchalant and landing somewhere between *cute* and *mildly unhinged.*

The man raised an eyebrow, his voice low and rich. "You'll survive."

I blinked. "Excuse me?"

He turned slightly, facing me fully now. Up close, he was all clean lines and quiet power—sharp jaw, stubble just edging into dangerous, and a suit that definitely cost more than my rent.

"You don't seem like the type who needs anyone to rush to your rescue," he said, voice smooth but clipped. Controlled.

"I'm not." I raised an eyebrow. "But I *am* the type who notices when men pretend they weren't raised by someone who taught them how to stand in line."

That made him smirk. Barely. A little twitch at the corner of his mouth like he wasn't used to being challenged, and maybe—*just maybe*—he liked it.

The bartender finally made eye contact. "What can I get you?"

"Vodka lemonade. Heavy on the vodka, light on the mansplaining," I said, loud enough for him to hear it.

The man huffed a quiet laugh. "Spirited."

I shrugged. "Or just sober enough to be done with everyone's bullshit."

He lifted his glass slightly, like a toast. "To being done."

I hesitated. Clinked my glass against his. "To being done."

We drank in silence.

He didn't ask my name. I didn't ask his. But the air between us buzzed with something I didn't have words for yet.

He glanced down at my hand, then back at my face. "That ring on your middle finger... doesn't suit you."

I looked down. Simple silver band, nothing special. "And why's that?"

"It looks like armor," he said. "You don't strike me as someone who hides behind metal."

My breath caught.

Before I could come up with a halfway decent response, he nodded toward the bartender, then straightened, pulling a phone from his pocket. The moment shifted—slipping away like smoke.

"I'll let you get back to your friends," he said, already turning.

And just like that—he was gone.

I stared after him for a second too long, heart still doing cartwheels like a drunk cheerleader.

Rachel's voice popped up behind me, smug and amused. "Oh, *that's* dangerous."

I didn't answer. My mouth had stopped working somewhere between "spirited" and "armor."

Whoever he was... I had a feeling that was *not* the last time I'd see him.

The drink hit faster than I expected. Or maybe it was the stare—*his* stare—that sent the heat rising in my chest.

I slipped back to the booth, and Rachel gave me a look that was one part "spill the tea" and two parts "did he propose?"

Maya didn't even bother with subtlety. "You looked like you were either going to slap him or kiss him. Which is it?"

"I don't know," I said truthfully. "But I wouldn't mind doing both."

They laughed. Rachel downed the rest of her drink and jumped to her feet. "Enough lurking. Time to dance."

Ten minutes later, we were in the middle of the dance floor, surrounded by bodies and bass. The music was loud, the lights low, and for the first time in seven weeks, I felt good. Not whole. Not healed. But alive.

I closed my eyes, letting the rhythm pull me in.

When I opened them again, my gaze swept toward the bar—and there he was. Still there. Still watching.

Not openly. Not obviously. But I caught it. The way his eyes tracked my every move. The way his jaw tightened when I rolled my hips to the beat. The way he sipped his drink like it was the only thing keeping him from doing something entirely reckless.

So, naturally, I turned it up.

I let my hands skim down my sides, moved closer to Rachel and Maya, leaned back and laughed at something Maya said that I didn't even hear. Every movement was deliberate. I was putting on a show, and he was the audience.

Another drink found its way into my hand. Then another.

Eventually, Rachel and Maya disappeared into a group of men who looked like they owned boats and couldn't spell "emotional maturity."

I stood alone at the edge of the dance floor, heart racing, skin buzzing.

And then I saw him again—still at the bar, still unreadable.

I didn't think. I didn't plan.

I just walked.

He noticed me immediately, his eyes locking on mine as I

crossed the room. I half expected him to look away, to pretend like earlier hadn't happened.

He didn't.

I slid into the empty space beside him, heartbeat drumming a wild rhythm against my ribs.

"I'm not usually this bold," I said, settling my glass on the counter like it was a dare.

His mouth twitched. "You sure about that?"

"Not at all."

He tilted his head, studied me with that same calm intensity that made my spine tingle. "You dance like you're trying to start a riot."

I smiled, slow and deliberate. "And you watch like you're trying to put one out."

Another toast. Another clink. Another unspoken challenge hanging between us like smoke.

I didn't know who he was.

But I knew one thing for sure:

This man was dangerous.

And I was already too far gone to care.

4

Chapter 4

Lexi

I should have walked away.

That would've been the sensible thing—finish my drink, flash a polite smile, return to my friends, and bask in the safety of a booth full of women who wouldn't wreck me on sight.

But I didn't.

Instead, I tilted my head, studying the man in front of me. The way his broad frame leaned into the bar like it owed him rent. The slow, controlled way he brought his whiskey to his lips. And God help me, the sharp, masculine edge of his jaw made my fingers twitch with the stupid, reckless urge to trace it.

"You never told me your name," I said, swirling the ice in my glass like it could cool the fire steadily crawling up my spine.

His lips curved—*barely*. It wasn't a smile. It was something more dangerous. "Neither did you."

"Maybe I like the mystery."

He didn't laugh. He didn't even blink. He just looked at me

like he could see through my dress, my bravado, my entire post-breakup spiral.

"Maybe I do too," he said, voice low and smooth, like the kind of sin you'd only commit in candlelight.

I took a sip of my drink and felt it settle in my chest like courage. "You ever do something completely out of character?"

That got his attention. His brow ticked upward, just enough to make it feel like a dare. "Occasionally."

I set my glass down and leaned in slightly, watching the way his gaze flicked down, then back to my face with the kind of focus that made my skin hum.

"I just got out of a relationship. A bad one."

His eyes didn't soften. They sharpened.

"And I decided—just for once—that I should do something reckless."

The silence between us tightened, like the pause before lightning strikes. He straightened slightly, the muscle in his jaw flexing.

"One night," I continued. "No names. No strings. Just... a distraction."

He stared at me. Not the casual kind. The kind that made me feel like I'd just been put under a microscope. He didn't look surprised. He looked like he'd expected this from me.

But still—he waited.

Then he exhaled a breath that could've passed for a laugh in a darker room, and took another sip of his drink. "You sure you can handle that?"

I raised an eyebrow. "Because I'm younger?"

His mouth curved again, but his eyes didn't lose their edge. "Because you look like you don't know how dangerous that could be."

I leaned in just enough to tip the balance. "Maybe I'm not as soft as I look."

His knuckles whitened slightly around the glass. And then, without breaking eye contact, he reached into his jacket, pulled out a black keycard, and slid it across the bar like it was the most casual sin in the world.

"Top floor," he murmured, voice just rough enough to scrape along my spine. "If you're serious."

My heart stuttered. I stared down at the keycard like it had teeth.

He didn't explain. He didn't chase. He just waited—like a man who didn't ask for anything, because he already knew what people would give him.

I met his gaze, fingers closing around the card. "Give me five minutes."

He didn't smile. Just gave a single, devastating nod.

I turned, heels clicking like a countdown, adrenaline pounding behind my ribs as I pushed back into the crowd.

Back on the dance floor, the lights were dizzying, the music loud. But all I could feel was the heavy press of the keycard against my hip—and the ghost of his voice in my ear.

Rachel spotted me and grabbed my hand. "Where'd you disappear to?"

"Just getting a drink," I said, faking casual like it was my job.

Maya raised a brow. "You always come back looking like you got offered a role in a thriller and a lap dance at the same time?"

I laughed, too quickly. "I'm calling it a night. The drink's hitting harder than expected."

Rachel frowned. "Already? We just got here."

"I know. I just... need sleep more than another round."

Maya studied me, then slowly nodded. "Sure. But if you *are* sneaking off to do something scandalous, blink twice."

"I'll text you," I said, grinning.

They hugged me goodbye, offered veiled threats about demanding details in the morning, and just like that—I was moving toward the exit.

The night air hit me like a reset button. Cold. Crisp. Real.

But the keycard in my hand said none of this was real. Not in the morning. Not in a week. Not when I inevitably returned to my regular, broken, overthinking self.

Tonight wasn't about healing.

It was about *burning.*

And I had just lit the match.

5

Chapter 5

Lexi

The elevator ride to the top floor was quiet—almost too quiet. No music. No small talk. Just the sound of my pulse pounding in my ears and the keycard clutched in my fingers like a secret I hadn't decided whether to keep or destroy.

When the doors slid open, I stepped into silence. Plush carpet, dim lighting, and the kind of hallway that whispered money. I walked, slow and deliberate, until I reached the suite. My hand hovered—ready to knock—but the door opened before I touched it.

He stood there like he'd been waiting. One hand braced against the frame, shirt unbuttoned just enough to be a threat. His tie was gone, his hair slightly tousled, like the night had already run its fingers through him. His eyes locked on mine— sharp, unreadable.

"You came," he said, voice low, rough around the edges.

I swallowed hard, stepping inside. He moved back without a word, letting me pass, then closed the door with a soft, final click. I was suddenly very aware of how alone we were. How big the room was. How close he stood.

"I don't usually do things like this," I said, my voice quiet, uncertain despite the heels and the makeup and the dress I picked to make exes weep.

His gaze dragged over me slowly, unapologetically. "Good," he murmured, like it was a confession. "I like being the exception."

My breath caught. He stepped forward—close enough to feel, not quite close enough to touch.

"I need you to be sure," he said, fingers brushing my chin, tilting my face up until our eyes locked. "Because once I start—"

"I know," I cut in, my voice steadier than I felt. "I don't want you to stop."

The heat between us snapped taut.

He growled—*actually growled*—and then his mouth was on mine, urgent, claiming, like he'd been holding back for far too long. There was no preamble. No hesitancy. Just teeth, tongue, heat, and need. His hands were in my hair, then on my waist, then gripping me like I might disappear.

He kissed like he fought—strategic, intense, devastating.

Then he broke away just enough to speak, voice rough against my cheek. "Tell me you want this."

"I do," I breathed. "I want you."

His eyes flared. Like that was the switch.

His hands slid beneath the hem of my dress, fingertips grazing along my spine, memorizing me. He didn't rush. He *learned*—the way I moved, the way I shivered under his touch, the way I gasped when his mouth found my throat.

When he reached the zipper, he paused. I hesitated, instinctively folding my arms across my body as the dress began to slip.

He stopped me, gently but firmly taking my wrists and lowering them to my sides. His eyes never left mine.

"Don't hide from me," he said, voice like smoke and sin. "You're fucking perfect."

I should've laughed, deflected, made a joke. But I couldn't. Not under that gaze. Not with my skin buzzing and my brain short-circuiting.

The dress hit the floor.

And then he sank to his knees.

His mouth followed his hands, slow and reverent and merciless. He licked, nipped, and sucked his way down my body, unhurried and precise, tasting every inch of skin like it was his to claim. By the time he reached my thighs, my legs were shaking. And then—his tongue found my clit, and all coherent thought vanished. He didn't just touch—he devoured. Worshipped. Like I was something holy, and he was finally allowed to believe in something again.

Pleasure bloomed, hot and overwhelming, as his tongue worked slow circles over my clit, alternating between gentle laps and sharp, sucking pressure that sent my body arching into him. He slid two fingers inside me, curling just right, dragging a cry from my throat I hadn't even known I was capable of. His free hand gripped my thigh, holding me open, holding me still, while his mouth drove me higher—licking, flicking, tasting until I was trembling, moaning, coming undone against his face. My knees buckled and I had to cling to the wall just to stay standing. He held me through it—speaking words I didn't understand, murmured in Russian, but they sank deep anyway.

"Beg for me, kotyonok," he whispered, and I did. I begged. I let go.

And he *didn't stop.*

When it became too much—when I was shaking, breathless, undone—he lifted me effortlessly and carried me to the bed like I weighed nothing. He laid me down with a gentleness that made the hunger in his eyes feel all the more dangerous.

Standing at the edge, he undid his belt—slow, deliberate, controlled. Every move designed to undo me. He reached into the drawer beside the bed without breaking eye contact, pulled out a condom, and tore the foil with practiced ease. It was careful. Intimate. Considerate in a way that made the heat in my chest flare even hotter.

I swallowed hard. "I have an IUD," I said softly. "And I'm clean."

His eyes darkened, a flicker of something unreadable passing through them before he shook his head slightly. "I've never been bare with anyone," he said, quiet but firm. "Not once."

Then, without breaking eye contact, he rolled the condom on with deliberate, practiced ease—still controlled, still composed, like even this was something he did with purpose.

He climbed onto the bed, lowered himself until we were nose to nose. "Look at me."

I did.

And when he slid into me, slow and thick and impossibly deep, I felt it in every nerve ending I'd ever owned. He was big—more than I was ready for, stretching me open with every inch, forcing my body to accommodate him with a tight, almost unbearable squeeze that bordered on pain and pleasure. My breath hitched, my back arched, and I clung to him, adjusting around the overwhelming fullness of him.

We moved together like we'd done this a thousand times. Like we were made for it. There was nothing frantic about it— just deep, grinding tension. Every thrust a promise. Every kiss a command. I forgot everything—names, pasts, consequences. All I knew was this.

Him.

Me.

The way he held my hips like he could shape me to fit him.

The way he whispered Russian into my neck like it was sacred.

The way he *needed* this.

And when I came, it was like falling—fast and hard and endless. He followed with a sound that felt pulled from somewhere primal, holding me like I was the only real thing in the world.

After, we stayed tangled together. Breathing. Shaking. Real.

I should've felt vulnerable. Exposed. Scared.

Instead, I felt... seen.

And I didn't know what that meant.

But I knew this wasn't over.

Not even close.

6

Chapter 6

Lexi

The first thing I noticed was the sunlight slipping through the hotel curtains, painting the suite in soft gold. The room was quiet, warm, and still. For a few seconds, I let myself just exist in it. No expectations. No reality.

Then the memories hit—slow and cinematic. The sound of his voice, low and dangerous. His hands on my skin. The way he looked at me like I was something rare, something he hadn't let himself want in a long time.

I turned my head, heart stuttering.

He was still asleep.

Laid out on his stomach, head buried in the pillow, hair a mess, his back bare and broad and breathtaking. The sheet had slipped low around his hips, and for one insane second I thought about staying. Curling against him. Running my fingers down the muscles of his spine like last night had never ended.

But that would mean opening a door I wasn't ready to walk

through.

I slid out of bed slowly, my legs still a little shaky, the ache between them a quiet, pulsing reminder of just how real last night had been. My dress was where I'd left it—a crumpled heap of poor decisions and amazing memories. I pulled it on carefully, wincing as I smoothed it over my skin.

No shoes. Whatever. I could survive barefoot.

As I moved around the room, I saw him stir slightly but didn't stop. I wasn't going to wake him. Not because I was afraid— but because I didn't trust myself not to stay.

I grabbed the hotel's paper notepad, paused, then scribbled a line that felt casual enough to mask the emotional hangover creeping in.

Thanks for the most spontaneous night of my life. You were epic.

I hesitated before adding the last line.

Maybe one day our paths will cross again.

I set it on the pillow beside him.

He didn't move.

And I didn't look back as I slipped out the door.

* * *

Rachel was already halfway through her coffee when I stepped into the apartment, barefoot, mascara definitely not where I left it last night.

She looked up from her mug like a cat that had cornered a mouse. "Well, well, well. And here I thought you got kidnapped by a really polite cult."

"Good morning to you too," I said, tossing my shoes into the hallway basket.

She squinted. "You're walking funny. That's a good sign."

I groaned. "Do you *ever* not go for the throat before break-fast?"

Rachel grinned. "Nope. Spill."

I collapsed onto the couch. My whole body still hummed. I tried to downplay it, but I couldn't keep the smile from tugging at my mouth. "It was... intense."

"Older guy, yes? Tall, broody, suspiciously good with his hands?"

"Yes, yes, and *yes.*"

Rachel pointed triumphantly. "I *knew* it. You've got that post-life-changing-sex glow."

I rolled my eyes. "It was just one night. No names."

Her eyes widened. "Lexi."

"It's fine. That was the deal. One night. No strings."

She crossed her arms, grinning like the villain she absolutely was. "You're already thinking about him again, aren't you?"

I stared at the ceiling.

Yeah. I definitely was.

7

Chapter 7

Lexi

I don't know what I expected after a night like that.

An epiphany? An emotional breakthrough? A vision quest led by an aggressively sexy Russian man?

Instead, I got Sunday night.

And the full, looming weight of Monday.

After four months off—four blissful, unstructured months of avoiding ex-boyfriends, emotionally bankrupt forwards, and emails from sponsors—it was back to work tomorrow. The off-season was officially over, and the first day of training camp was staring at me like a looming punishment from the hockey gods.

The season was only a few weeks away. Which meant the chaos was about to restart.

Back to early mornings. Rink-side caffeine. Photoshoots with players who hated smiling. And pretending like my life wasn't held together with dry shampoo and vibes.

I lay on the couch with a hoodie pulled over my head like a

fabric exorcism, still soft and sore in places that reminded me *exactly* what I'd been doing the night before.

Unfortunately, Rachel wouldn't let me mope in peace.

"Any updates from Midnight Daddy?" she called from the kitchen.

I groaned into the cushion. "We are not calling him that."

"What about Mystery Man? Coach Dreamboat? That one has range and you are clearly obsessed."

I pulled the pillow over my face. "I'm not obsessed."

"Mmhmm. That's why you're sighing like a lovesick regency heroine."

I gave up trying to win and dragged myself toward the bathroom. The shower was scalding—part cleanse, part penance. I tried to wash him off, but he was still there, burned into my skin. His voice. His hands. The way he looked at me like he already knew how I'd fall apart.

I leaned against the shower wall, eyes shut, and whispered, "It was just one night."

Like if I said it enough, it would stop feeling like a lie.

Afterward, I toweled off, threw on the biggest hoodie I owned, and shuffled back to my room like a ghost with Wi-Fi. My laptop sat on the desk, judging me. I opened it, fully bracing for inbox doom.

Emails. So many emails.

Sponsors. Practice schedules. Brand coordination. A few preseason PR reminders from the team's comms director, including an all-caps message that just said, "NO MORE SWEATY THIRST TRAPS OF HOCKEY PLAYERS."

Noted.

Buried halfway down the staff memo list was something new.

Please welcome the temporary interim head coach starting this week. Mandatory team introductions Monday. Yes, Lexi, this means you too. No social experiments.

Ugh. Probably another clipboard-wielding ex-player who thought Instagram was a personality flaw.

I flagged the message, made a mental note to fake enthusiasm, and closed the laptop with more force than necessary.

I laid back on the bed and stared at the ceiling. It used to feel like a reset—new season, new energy. But now? Something felt...off.

Maybe it was the silence that had followed last night.

Or the way my skin still buzzed like it remembered his touch too well.

Or the fact that I'd left without even asking his name, and yet my brain had replayed his voice like a favourite song on loop all day.

I pulled the blanket up to my chin, whispered to the dark, "One night. That's it."

And maybe, if I said it enough times, I'd actually believe it.

But I didn't.

Not even close.

8

Chapter 8

Lexi

The arena smelled like fresh paint, sweat, and regret.

A perfectly cursed blend of new beginnings and old trauma.

I stood just inside the staff entrance, clutching my coffee like it was the only thing keeping me from evaporating. The industrial lights buzzed faintly overhead, flickering like even the building wasn't sure it wanted to be awake yet. Same, honestly.

Four months off sounded like heaven in theory. Paid time to "regroup," "recharge," "get my head on straight." Cute. What it actually did was turn me into a reclusive, emotional raccoon who answered emails at 2 a.m. and cried at that one dog food commercial with the rescue pit bull and the violin music. I was feral and unfit for society.

But today wasn't about emotional instability. Today was about being professional. Focused. Normal.

Today was about walking into this place like I hadn't spontaneously combusted in the middle of a very public breakup, gotten humiliated by a professional athlete with the emotional depth of a cereal box, and had to move in with my childhood best friend to avoid spiralling into permanent couch-mode.

Back to work. Back to hockey. Back to the job I loved—even if the thought of Ethan's stupid face appearing somewhere in the building made me want to legally change my name and flee the country under witness protection.

I walked the familiar halls, each step echoing just a little too loudly, like even the floor remembered the drama. A couple interns passed by, both of them clutching clipboards and looking like they were one misplaced comma away from a nervous breakdown. I gave them a polite nod, trying to radiate "senior staff" and not "emotionally unstable woman on the verge of making PR someone else's problem."

The team's preseason meetings were already underway. The actual players weren't due for another week, which meant today was just media, PR, coaching staff, and the pre-chaos chaos. A warm-up round for the real storm.

My phone buzzed as I approached the elevator.

MAYA: *First day back and you better not already look like a Pinterest board titled "Anxious but Employed."*

MAYA: *You wearing that cursed hoodie again?*

I rolled my eyes and typed back with one hand.

ME: *It's comforting and it smells like competence, leave me alone.*

MAYA: *You say "comforting," I say "washed in your tears."*

MAYA: *You make it in yet?*

I hit the elevator button and texted back.

ME: *Just walked in. Pray for me.*

33

> **MAYA:** *Oh girl. I've been praying since I saw the staff memo.*
> **MAYA:** *Also... get ready. There's a* vibe *today.*
> **ME:** *That's not cryptic at all.*
> **MAYA:** *You'll see. Oh gods, you'll see.*

We'd started here together two years ago—just two over-caffeinated nobodies in a sea of team jackets and testosterone. She was the only one who made my job feel survivable. The kind of person who would drag you out of a bad date *and* a bad mental spiral with the same energy. She knew everything—about Ethan, about the breakup, and definitely about the mistake I was still trying to file under "Forgettable Decisions" and not "Unpaid Emotional Internship."

> The elevator dinged, and I stepped inside.
> One day back.
> I could do this.
> No emotional breakdowns.
> No drama.
> Just coffee, preseason planning, and probably pretending not to remember how to use half the scheduling software.
> My phone buzzed again just as the doors closed.
> **MAYA:** *Seriously. Brace yourself.*

Great.

The boardroom was already buzzing when I walked in—half-full coffee cups, media lanyards, and someone aggressively arguing with a printer in the corner.

Maya had saved me a seat with a post-it note that said **"Sit,**

peasant." Classic.

I slid into the chair beside her and offered a tight smile to the cluster of staffers I hadn't seen in months. Everyone looked a little tanner, a little more caffeinated, and a lot more ready for this season than I felt.

"Morning," Maya said under her breath. "Still got that 'I slept with a mysterious stranger' glow. Bold move."

"Still got that 'I live for chaos' energy," I shot back, sipping my coffee.

The room shifted around us—people settling, conversations fading. I glanced up to see our GM, Peter Langford, step forward to address the room.

"Alright," he said, voice smooth, rehearsed. "Let's get started. First of all, welcome back. I hope everyone had a relaxing, drama-free summer—because that's over now."

A few laughs. Some groans.

"And," he continued, "I'd like to introduce you to someone who'll be a key part of our leadership team this season. He'll be taking over as interim head coach while we finalize the permanent hire."

He paused, gesturing toward the doorway.

And then—

He walked in.

The man from the bar.

From the hotel.

From my skin.

From my dreams.

He strode into the room like he *owned it.* Like he'd never done anything as awkward as sleep with someone and then show up at their job without warning.

Black tailored suit. Clean shave. Not a hair out of place.

35

Not a trace of the man who'd begged me to look at him while he—

My brain *flatlined.*

Our eyes met.

And something passed between us—something thick and invisible and completely, utterly undeniable.

I didn't move. I didn't breathe.

His expression didn't flicker. Not even a muscle twitched.

He nodded to the room, calm and collected, the very picture of professional control.

Peter's voice cut through the fog in my head.

"This is James Volkov," he said. "He's coming on temporarily to help lead the team through pre-season. Most of you know his career history—former player, championship coach, and, frankly, one of the most respected minds in the league."

James.

Volkov.

The name hit like a slap.

I hadn't asked for his name.

He hadn't offered.

And now it had a face. A job. A title.

His gaze scanned the room casually—until it landed on me.

And stayed there.

Not long. Just enough. Just long enough for my soul to leave my body and file an HR complaint.

I felt the heat crawl up my neck. I looked down. Pretended my coffee was suddenly the most interesting thing in the world.

Maya leaned over and whispered, "Tell me that's not him."

I didn't respond.

Because it was.

Peter moved on, droning through the rest of the announcements like he hadn't just handed my nervous system over to a human earthquake in a suit.

James—*James*—took a seat at the far end of the table, diagonally across from me. Not close enough to talk. Just close enough to haunt me.

He sat with effortless authority, fingers laced together on the table like he hadn't used them to ruin me two nights ago. His expression was unreadable. Professional. Aloof.

And still—*those eyes.*

I stared at my notepad like it contained state secrets. I could feel Maya watching me like a scientist observing a particularly juicy lab experiment.

Peter wrapped up with a painfully long-winded update on team branding initiatives, and then—

"Any questions before we break for department leads to meet with Coach Volkov?"

My pen slipped.

Maya snorted.

James's gaze flicked to me like he *heard* it.

Peter gestured toward him. "James, anything you'd like to say before we divide into groups?"

James stood, slow and deliberate. He adjusted the cuffs of his jacket like he was prepping for a photoshoot—or maybe a duel. I couldn't tell which.

"Just one thing," he said smoothly, voice deep and calm and dangerously familiar. "I look forward to working closely with everyone. Especially our media and PR team."

My soul briefly attempted to vacate my body.

His eyes slid to mine.

Maya audibly gasped, then turned it into a cough so theatrical it could've earned an Oscar.

I forced a smile. "Oh, we're a delight. Can't wait to... work closely."

His mouth twitched. *Just barely.* "I'm counting on it."

Was it hot in here? No? Just the flaming wreckage of my sanity.

Peter, who apparently had no idea we were two seconds from spontaneously combusting, nodded. "Great. Let's break out."

Chairs scraped. Conversations resumed. James sat again, but not before giving me one last look—sharp and unreadable.

Maya leaned in so hard she was practically in my lap. "You had *sex* with the head coach?"

"Shhh."

"You had *anonymous, hotel-suite, life-altering* sex with our *new boss*."

"I didn't know!"

"Lexi."

"I didn't ask his name!"

"Oh my God."

I shoved my folder into my bag like that would solve anything. "This is fine."

"This is *not* fine."

"I'm going to act normal."

Maya blinked. "Babe. You are physically incapable of acting normal. You blush when someone says 'spreadsheet.'"

I stood up. "I'm a professional."

James stood too.

Our eyes met again.

He nodded—*just slightly.*

I walked out of the room like it wasn't collapsing around me.

9

Chapter 9

Lexi

By mid-afternoon, I had answered exactly three emails, ignored twelve, and rewritten the same press release intro four
times.

I kept trying to focus on work, but my brain had been melted
into useless soup by the Boardroom Incident. The name. The
voice. The *man*.

James Volkov.

And of course—because the universe was a petty little
gremlin—my office was freezing, and I'd forgotten my backup
hoodie. So I was sitting at my desk, shivering and spiraling in
a tank top, trying to act like I wasn't one "Hi, Lexi" away from
combusting.

A soft knock at the doorframe.

I looked up.

And there he was.

Leaning casually against the door, arms crossed, like he had every right to be standing there. Like he didn't look too good in that dark navy dress shirt. Like he hadn't ruined me with his hands two nights ago and then introduced himself to my boss.

"Busy?" he asked, voice low and way too familiar.

My spine straightened. "Oh, you know. Just working. On work. Like a person who works here. Because I do."

He raised an eyebrow, clearly amused. "Impressive sentence structure."

"Didn't realize grammar was part of your coaching style."

He stepped inside without asking.

My brain short-circuited.

He closed the door behind him.

My soul briefly attempted to leave through the air vent.

"I thought we agreed," I said, standing to put some distance between us, "that this was a one-time thing."

"I don't remember agreeing to anything," he replied, slow and controlled. "You left before we could... debrief."

I blinked. "Did you just make a *post-hookup strategy meeting* sound like an actual playbook?"

"You're the one who said no names, no strings."

I folded my arms. "And you're the one who showed up at my job like a plot twist I did *not* request."

He stepped closer—just enough to make my skin buzz.

"I didn't know," he said. "If I had, I might've thought twice."

I searched his face for any sign he was lying. He wasn't.

That was the worst part.

It wasn't some twisted power move. It was just... fate. Horrible, hot, HR-violating fate.

"I'm your PR manager," I said. "I'm literally in charge of

your public image."

His mouth curved, slow and deliberate. "Then I'm in good hands."

I turned away, because looking at him was dangerous. Like staring into the sun if the sun was six-foot-two and smelled like expensive regret.

He didn't move.

"You left a note," he said, voice softer now. "Most people don't."

I shrugged, keeping my back to him. "Most people don't ruin me in one night."

Silence.

Then, quietly: "It wasn't just one night for me."

That did it. I turned to face him—and he was closer than I realized. Close enough that if I leaned forward, I could count the flecks of steel in his eyes. Close enough that I could feel the heat rolling off him.

I didn't move.

Neither did he.

The air between us crackled.

His gaze dropped to my mouth.

My breath caught.

Then—before I could think, before I could talk myself out of it—*I kissed him.*

Or maybe he kissed me.

I didn't know who moved first. It didn't matter. His mouth crashed into mine with the kind of desperation you only feel when you've spent the entire day pretending you don't want someone.

My back hit the desk.

His hands were everywhere—firm, confident, sliding over

my waist like he owned the moment. I gasped as he lifted me, set me on the edge of the desk like I weighed nothing, like he *knew* exactly how to ruin me all over again.

I grabbed his shirt, pulling him closer, my legs instinctively wrapping around his waist. His hands slid up my thighs, heat flooding my skin, mouth devouring mine like he couldn't get enough.

I should have stopped it.

I *meant* to stop it.

But when he groaned against my neck and whispered, "God, I've been thinking about this since you left—"

I froze.

And that was all it took.

Reality slammed back in.

This wasn't some hotel suite. This was work. *My* job. *His* job. And we were two seconds away from defiling my keyboard.

I shoved against his chest—firm, but not panicked. Not quite.

He stepped back instantly, breathing hard, hands still hovering at my sides like he didn't want to let go.

"I can't," I said, voice shaking just enough to sting. "I'm not that girl. Not at work. And definitely not... not with anyone in hockey."

His eyes flickered—just briefly—but he didn't ask. Didn't press.

Smart man.

I slid off the desk and turned away, running a hand through my hair and trying to remember how to breathe like a person who hadn't just made out with her boss.

"I'm sorry," I muttered, not sure if I meant it.

James was quiet for a beat. Then he said, softly, "You kissed me first."

I turned my head. "Yeah. I also stopped it."

Another pause.

Then: "You're not the only one trying to be professional."

He left before I could say anything else. Before I could figure out whether I wanted him to.

The door clicked shut.

And I sat back down in my chair, heart pounding, lips still tingling, and every part of me screaming the same thing:

This is going to be a problem.

10

Chapter 10

Lexi

I didn't even take my shoes off when I got home.

I just dropped my keys, kicked the door shut, and walked straight into my apartment like I was trying to outrun the memory of his mouth on mine and my body on my desk.

My actual desk.

At work.

Where I work.

I yanked off my jacket and paced my living room like I was trying to wear a hole in the floor. My phone was already in my hand, thumbs flying before my brain caught up.

GROUP CHAT: *Chaos Coven* 🔥🗡️

Lexi: *I did something stupid. Like, monumentally stupid. Like "please tell me I have blackmail material on both of you so you can never repeat this" stupid.*

Rachel: *IS THIS ABOUT COACH VOLKOV BECAUSE*

I'VE BEEN WAITING ALL DAY TO BE RIGHT – CANT BELIEVE HE IS YOUR SECRET HOOK UP!!!!

Maya: *Oh gods. Please tell me you didn't bang him in the Zamboni garage.*

Lexi: *No. Worse. My office.*

Rachel: YOUR OFFICE???

Maya: *Oh this is better than reality TV. Start from the top. Use vivid language.*

Lexi: *He came in to "talk." We bantered. There was tension. One thing led to another and next thing I know I'm sitting on my desk like a sexy HR violation.*

Rachel: ✂I✂am✂SO✂PROUD✂

Maya: *Tell me there was wall touching.   I need DETAILS, Michelson.*

Lexi: *We kissed. He was... Ugh. He was him.*

Rachel: *So... hot and broody and way too calm for someone who made you forget your own name in a hotel?*

Lexi: *Exactly. And then I stopped it. Told him I don't do this. Not at work. Not with* hockey people.

Rachel: *...ah.*

Maya: *Ohhhh. You said "not with hockey people." That was a capital-M Moment.*

Lexi: *I didn't say why, okay? But I think he clocked something. He's smart. Annoyingly observant.*

Rachel: *Okay but like... are we mad at you? Or kind of thrilled?*

Maya: *I'm emotionally invested and morally neutral.*

Lexi: *I just... don't want this to be a* thing. *It can't be a thing. I need this job. I like this job. And he's... him. And it's too messy.*

Rachel: *So you're definitely seeing him again.*

Maya: *Oh yeah. This is how the best emotional disasters start.*

I collapsed onto my couch, still in my work clothes, heels dangling off one foot and hair barely staying in the world's saddest ponytail. The fridge hummed in the background like it had advice. It didn't.

I stared at the screen, heart racing—and not in a cute "is he texting me?" way. More in a "congratulations, you've made the dumbest mistake with the hottest man alive" way.

Because the worst part was...

They were right.

I *was* going to see him again.

Tomorrow. And the day after that. And every day until this season got off the ground or I spontaneously combusted.

I closed the chat, let the phone fall to the couch beside me, and pulled my knees up to my chest.

It wasn't just the kiss.

It was the way he looked at me.

Like he already knew I wasn't done with him.

Like he *wasn't* done with me.

11

Chapter 11

Lexi

The next few days passed in a blur of preseason madness—sponsor calls, marketing deadlines, last-minute photo shoots, and Maya dragging me into at least three separate "creative brainstorms" that were really just thinly veiled gossip sessions.

And somehow, miraculously, I managed to avoid James entirely.

No hallway run-ins. No office drop-bys. Not even a brooding silhouette near the rink.

It felt... almost safe.

But of course, my luck had an expiration date.

Because today, he was here.

In the meeting. In the seat three chairs down. In the room where I had to pretend I hadn't kissed him, hadn't let him lift me onto my desk, hadn't moaned into his mouth like a woman with no boundaries or basic professionalism.

So, naturally, I was sweating through my bra.

The conference room was aggressively beige.

Beige walls, beige chairs, beige coffee in the sad communal carafe. It was the kind of room designed to make bold ideas die and dreams give up halfway through a PowerPoint.

I was trying to focus.

Truly. Deeply. Trying.

But James was three seats down.

Perfect posture. Suit jacket folded neatly over the back of his chair. Hands clasped loosely in front of him like he wasn't the living, breathing source of my current unravelling.

He hadn't looked at me once.

Which, honestly, felt like its own kind of war.

Meanwhile, Maya was sitting diagonally across from me, sipping iced coffee and texting with the subtlety of a neon sign.

Maya:

He hasn't looked at you once.

That means he's thinking about it non-stop.

Classic repression.

Lexi:

STOP.

I'm trying to be normal.

Professional. Chill.

Like an adult who didn't make out with their boss on company furniture.

Maya:

You are not chill.

You look like you're trying to astral project out of your

own body.

Peter, blissfully unaware, was talking through preseason branding plans. Something about new uniforms, social campaigns, player media training. I nodded, scribbled a note, and definitely didn't write "STOP LOOKING SO GOOD" in the margins.

James finally spoke.

"Will we be integrating real-time content into training sessions? Or keeping those scheduled around media availability?"

I jumped.

His voice was deeper than I remembered. Or maybe it was the room. Or the fact that I was on the verge of spontaneously combusting.

Peter gestured to me. "Lexi, thoughts?"

I cleared my throat, definitely not choking on my own anxiety. "Uh, yes. We're planning a few livestreamed segments during practice once camp is in full swing. 'Behind the Boards' style content. But we'll keep media day clean for sponsored coverage."

James nodded, but there was something in his expression.

Something knowing.

Something like, *I remember exactly how your voice sounds when you're lying.*

I hated him.

I hated him and his face and the way my body still remembered his hands on my thighs.

Maya:
Did you see that? That was eye contact.
That was "I've touched your soul and other places"

eye contact.
Lexi:
Blocked.
Reported.
Unsubscribed.

The meeting dragged on. Notes were taken. Ideas pitched. Coffee consumed. And the whole time, I could feel the tension building—like we were both pretending this was normal.

It wasn't.

Finally, as people started packing up, Peter turned to James. "You'll have a chance to meet more of the players next week once the vets are back in town. I'll introduce you to the newer guys sooner."

James nodded. "Looking forward to it."

Then, for the first time since I walked in, he looked at me.

Really looked at me.

And said, "And Lexi? I'll need a one-on-one later this week. Just to go over public-facing content strategy."

His tone was polite. Professional.

His eyes were *not*.

I nodded slowly, keeping my face carefully blank. "Of course. Just let me know what time works for you."

Everyone started filing out.

Maya passed behind me and whispered, "You're so screwed."

And I was.

So, so screwed.

* * *

The past few days had been pure preseason madness—content deadlines, scheduling mishaps, two rookie interviews that somehow devolved into a full-blown Nerf war. I buried myself in work, buried my thoughts, buried everything I didn't want to admit was simmering beneath the surface.

I hadn't seen James since the day he showed up in my office.

No hallway run-ins. No dark looks. Not even a flash of tailored menace near the rink.

And still—I felt him everywhere.

In the tension that lived in my spine.

In the way my body flinched when someone said his name.

In the heat that bloomed every time I remembered the way he'd touched me, kissed me... *almost* ruined me.

Almost.

Until this morning.

Media/Strategy Sync – Volkov & Michelson

Conference Room 4B. 3:00PM.

No details. No warning. Just a time. A place. A test.

I stared at the glass door, checked my reflection—twice. I was perfectly composed. Completely unbothered. Professionally dressed and emotionally unavailable.

Liar.

I knocked once and stepped in.

He was already there.

Sitting at the far end of the table, sleeves rolled, top buttons undone, tie nowhere in sight. His gaze lifted to mine like I was right on time for something I hadn't agreed to.

"Lexi," he said. Smooth. Dark. Like he knew exactly what

I'd been avoiding.

"Coach Volkov," I replied, walking in with a clipboard I didn't need and a fantasy I refused to acknowledge.

"You're still going with that?" he asked, gaze tracking me as I took my seat across from him.

"It's professional," I said evenly.

"It's adorable," he murmured. "But we're well past professional, aren't we?"

My stomach tightened. I opened my laptop.

He didn't speak. Didn't move. Just let the silence thicken until I was the one cracking under it.

So I launched into the media strategy like it was a script. Season schedule. Social rollouts. Partner activations. I kept my voice calm, my hands steady, my breathing even.

And he just watched me.

Like a man watching fire crawl toward dry brush.

"You're good at this," he said when I paused. "You sound in control."

I met his gaze. "I am."

"You're not."

He stood.

Didn't circle. Didn't pace.

Just came toward me.

Slow. Intentional.

Like he already knew I wouldn't stop him.

He stopped at my side.

I didn't look at him.

But I could feel it—the shift. The gravity of him.

"Tell me," he said, voice low and razor-sharp, "is that why you wore that skirt? Control?"

My pulse stuttered.

I looked up.

Big mistake.

His eyes were darker than they had any right to be. Focused. Consuming.

"You want me to be professional?" he asked. "You came here thinking we'd talk strategy and leave untouched?"

"Didn't we agree to pretend nothing happened?" I said, voice tight.

"You can pretend."

His fingers brushed my knee.

"Me?" He leaned in. "I'm done pretending."

Then he kissed me.

Hard. Hot. Hands tangled in my hair and breath stolen in one devastating pull.

I gasped as he lifted me out of the chair, my back hitting the edge of the table in a clean sweep of motion that was way too smooth for something so reckless.

"You want gentle?" he growled against my throat.

"No."

"Good."

He turned me, lifted me onto the table, and pushed my knees apart like he was opening a door that had always belonged to him.

My skirt rode up. My blouse pulled loose. I tried to speak—tried to think—but his hands were already on me, everywhere at once, mapping every inch like he was remembering it.

When he pressed into me—deep, hard, unrelenting—I bit my lip to keep from crying out.

His pace was merciless.

Measured. Devastating.

Every thrust filled me completely, perfectly, like his body

had been built to shatter mine in all the right ways.

I clutched the edge of the table, the cold surface grounding me as my hips rocked to meet him, over and over again. There was no pause. No relief. Just his breath in my ear and his hands anchoring me in place.

"You feel that?" he growled. "That's what happens when you act like I didn't wreck you the first time."

I couldn't answer.

He kept going. Kept moving. Kept ruining me.

"Say my name."

"James—" I choked out.

"Louder."

"James."

His fingers slid under my jaw, tilting my face up until our eyes locked.

"I want you to remember this every time you try to walk past me like nothing happened."

My body was already unravelling, every nerve on fire, pressure coiling low in my stomach. And then—his hand between us, finding the spot that made me whimper.

It was over in seconds.

I came hard, breath ragged, legs trembling around him.

And still he didn't stop.

He kept going—chasing his own release with a force that left me boneless beneath him, his name still on my lips when he finally groaned, collapsing forward as he followed me over the edge.

The only sound in the room was our breathing.

He stayed like that for a moment—forehead pressed to mine, one hand still braced beside my head, the other curled possessively around my hip.

Then, slowly, he stepped back.

I blinked up at the ceiling, heart pounding in my chest, body wrecked, mouth dry.

He straightened his shirt.

I fixed my skirt.

No words were spoken.

Until—

"I'm not done with you," he said, eyes burning into mine. "Not even close."

And then he left.

Like he hadn't just broken me in half and made me want more.

12

Chapter 12

James

The locker room snapped to attention the second I stepped inside.

It wasn't loud. That's not how reverence worked in places like this. It was the sudden hush. The stretch of silence when voices dropped and eyes found the floor. Like the air had shifted and they couldn't explain why.

They knew who I was.

They'd watched me on screens growing up—jerseys, high-light reels, fights I won and goals I buried. I didn't need to say a word. My name did the talking.

"Morning," I said, low and even, cutting through the room like a blade.

A chorus of "Morning, Coach" followed, some confident, some nervous, one or two barely audible.

My eyes scanned the room. Players shifting, straightening up, a few nodding to each other with wide-eyed grins they were trying to suppress.

And then—

Ethan.

Leaning against the far wall, arms crossed.

No grin. No nod.

Just a tight jaw and a look like I'd personally insulted his bloodline by existing.

He didn't say anything.

Didn't move.

Didn't even blink when our eyes met.

Good. He wanted a war? Fine. I'd been fighting ghosts longer than he'd been alive.

I broke the stare first—not because I couldn't hold it, but because *he* needed to know I wasn't going to give him the satisfaction.

"Hit the ice in ten," I said. "Lines are posted. If you can't read, ask someone smarter."

Laughter. Tension broken. A few of the rookies visibly relaxed, like I wasn't about to grind them into the boards for the next six months.

I turned to check the lineup posted outside the coach's office, but she hit me first.

Not literally.

Lexi.

Just the thought of her name, and my hands curled into fists.

She'd been in my head for days—burned into the back of my skull like a scar that wouldn't stop throbbing. I still felt her thighs wrapped around me. The taste of her on my tongue. The way her eyes glazed over when I told her not to look away and she didn't.

She should've been a mistake. A one-time slip.

But nothing about her had slipped.

She *dug in.* Buried deep. Like she belonged under my skin.

And now I couldn't stop. Couldn't stop wondering where she was. What she was doing. Whether she still felt sore when she sat down at her desk.

My jaw clenched.

This wasn't like me. I didn't get distracted.

Not by anyone. Especially not someone who worked under me—someone who could burn everything down if I wasn't careful.

But all I wanted to do was find her.

See her face.

Hear her voice.

Touch her again.

I slammed the thought back down and walked toward the rink.

Halfway there, I heard it.

"Wait... no way. You and Wilson are related?"

The voice came from the direction of the locker room— young, dumb, too loud.

A pause.

And then the sound of every player in that room shutting up instantly.

I turned.

Ethan had stepped forward now, out from his corner. Eyes locked on the rookie who'd said it—Tanner, maybe? Some eager kid from Toronto who hadn't learned what silence was worth.

Ethan's voice was flat. Ice-cold. "Not related. He's just the guy who knocked up my mom and mailed it in."

Oof.

I didn't flinch.

I didn't show a damn thing.

I looked at him—really looked—and for one second, he looked exactly like I had at his age. Angry. Walled off. Sharp enough to cut anyone who got too close.

The room was frozen.

Tanner looked like he wanted to crawl into a gym bag and zip it closed.

Someone dropped their water bottle, and it echoed like a gunshot.

I just nodded once. "Enough talk. Gear up."

And then I walked out.

Because the only thing worse than saying the wrong thing... was saying anything at all.

* * *

I used to love this. The smell of the ice. The nerves. The routine of it all. But now? Every minute leading up to today had felt like sandpaper—necessary, gritty, and just uncomfortable enough to remind me why I came back.

Ethan.

My son. My mess. My maybe.

It had been years. Years of doing what I was told—staying away, sending checks, pretending distance was protection. His mother made it clear: stay gone, keep your legacy clean, and don't confuse him. She'd told me he was better off not knowing who I really was.

So I stayed gone. I kept skating. Signed endorsements. Played the part. Focused on goals, stats, contracts. Focused on *not thinking about him.*

But I thought about him every time I laced up. Every time

the cameras flashed. Every time I saw another kid wearing my number and wondered if he hated me for it.

The truth is, I don't know how to be a dad.

But I know I can't be a stranger anymore.

And if all I get is this season—just this one shot to stand on the same ice as him and prove I didn't forget—I'll take it. I'll take the hits, the looks, the fury he's got every right to feel.

Because I didn't come here to be liked.

I came here to be *known.*

13

Chapter 13

James

The rink was colder than usual.

Good. I needed it to be.

The second I stepped onto the ice, the noise dulled. Voices dropped. The scrape of skates and the snap of gear faded into a heavy kind of silence.

They were watching me.

Not just looking. *Watching.*

Some of these kids grew up with my name on the back of their jerseys. They knew the clips—my goals, my hits, my fists. They knew the stories.

The blood. The stats. The legend.

But none of that mattered now.

"Let's go!" I barked. "Two laps warm up—cut corners and you start over."

They moved. Fast.

The rookies scrambled to impress. The vets paced themselves, eyes always tracking me, waiting for tone, direction, weakness. There was none. I didn't believe in giving them that. You don't lead with softness. You earn that later—*maybe.*

I was halfway through watching line drills when I felt the shift.

Ethan. He was flying.

Not because he wanted to prove himself.

Because he wanted to make me watch.

Every move was sharp. Aggressive. Controlled rage disguised as effort.

He didn't glance at me once. But every puck he handled, every stop, every shove along the boards said what he wouldn't.

You don't belong here.

I stayed silent. Let him burn.

But when he cut off another player mid-rush, nearly taking a guy's legs out just to get to the puck first, I blew the whistle hard.

"Wilson! Off the line."

Ethan skidded to a stop, panting. Helmet pushed back. Eyes full of defiance.

I skated toward him, ignoring the tension in the air. The rest of the team had paused—awkward glances, frozen breath.

"You want to hit your own team mates? Go play football," I said.

"Just leading by example, Coach," he shot back, lips curling. "That's what you like, right? Leading from a distance?"

The jab landed. I didn't show it.

"Cut the attitude."

"I'm skating circles around everyone out here and you're coming for *me*? What, trying to make up for lost time one whistle at a time?"

My voice dropped. "You're out of line."

Ethan ripped his gloves off, let them drop. "You're out of *your* mind if you think I care."

We were chest to chest now. Not yelling. Just seething.

"You think you can walk in here and what—play Daddy? Earn my respect with drills and playbooks?"

"I didn't come to play anything," I snapped. "I came because I'm tired of hiding. Because your mother poisoned you against me and I'm done letting that be the story."

That got him.

His mouth parted like I'd punched him straight in the gut.

"You don't get to talk about her," he hissed. "You think I didn't ask where you were? Think I didn't want to know why you never called? She never even had to lie. You did that all on your own."

I stepped back, jaw tight.

"I sent money. Every month."

"Yeah, and I needed a dad, not a damn direct deposit." He shoved my shoulder. "You think writing checks gives you the right to be here?"

I didn't move. I let the shove land. Took it. Held it.

"You think I liked leaving?" I asked, low. "You think it didn't rip me in half? She lied to me. Manipulated everything. But I didn't come here to fix the past. I came because I *want to know you now.* Even if you fucking hate me for it."

He stared at me. Breathing hard. Red-faced. No more words left.

And that's when I felt it.

I turned—

She was stood watching us. Lexi.

Standing at the edge of the rink. Motionless. Haunted.

63

Her eyes bounced between us—me, then Ethan, then me again. Her lips parted slightly, like she was going to say something and couldn't. Like the oxygen had been vacuumed from her lungs.

She looked at Ethan.

And back to me.

And I saw it land.

Recognition.

Realization.

Everything in her face dropped. Like she'd just connected the dots she didn't know were there until they burned into her.

And I had no idea why.

No idea why she looked at me like I'd betrayed her.

14

Chapter 14

Lexi

I should've walked away.

The second I saw James on the ice, shouting orders like a king on a battlefield, I should've turned around.

But I didn't.

I stood behind the glass, half-hidden by the hallway wall, heart hammering in my throat. At first, it was just noise— skates slicing, players grunting, James barking commands that somehow made my knees weak.

And then—

"Wilson! Off the line."

I leaned closer, just enough to see the player in question. Tall. Blond. Familiar posture. Familiar anger.

Ethan.

My stomach bottomed out.

My feet didn't move. Couldn't.

They were yelling now. Their voices weren't hushed or hidden. Everyone on that ice could hear every word—and so could I.

"You think you can walk in here and what—play
Daddy?"

I blinked.
What??
No.
No.

"I came because I want to know you now. Even if you
fucking hate me for it."

And then I saw Ethan's face.
That face I used to kiss. That face I used to cry over.
And I looked back at James—
James, who had been inside me just days ago.
Who made me feel seen and wanted and ruined in the best
way.

"I needed you when I was five. Not now."

I couldn't breathe.
They were still going. Still unraveling.
James looked like he was barely holding himself together.
Ethan looked like he wanted to destroy something. And I—
I just stood there.
Frozen.
Watching it all collapse.
The man I'd been with.
The man I was still *aching* for.

The man I couldn't stop thinking about...

Was my ex's father.

I didn't move. Didn't breathe. Just listened as the air turned to ice and the weight of it all pressed down on my chest.

I wanted to scream. To disappear. To go back to before I ever walked into that bar.

But I didn't move.

Not when James turned toward me for a second and looked—shattered.

Not when Ethan shoved him and spit venom about how he'd been abandoned.

Not even when James said quietly, almost broken, *"Get off the ice."*

It wasn't until Ethan slammed his stick and stormed off, and the rest of the team slowly scattered like they'd just watched something sacred die...

That I finally let myself step back.

Just one step.

Then another.

The hallway spun around me like I was underwater, and I didn't realize I was walking until I reached the corridor behind the stands—cold and empty and quiet.

And then—

Footsteps. Fast. Heavy. Angry.

I froze again.

Ethan.

Coming straight at me.

I hadn't seen him since I caught him with that girl two months ago. Since he said *"It's not what it looks like"* with his shirt halfway on and her laughing behind him.

And now?

He blew right past me.

Didn't flinch.

Didn't speak.

Didn't even *look at me.*

Like I was invisible. Like I hadn't spent a year of my life trying to make that man happy. Like I didn't exist.

And that—

That hurt more than I thought it would.

I stood there, gut hollow, until I couldn't anymore. I ducked into the staff lounge, slammed the door, and locked it with shaking fingers.

And then I dropped.

Straight to the floor.

I didn't cry right away.

I just sat there, back to the door, knees pulled tight to my chest, heart thudding like it was trying to break through bone.

I had slept with his father.

I had fallen for his father.

And I didn't even know who that made me.

A horrible person?

An idiot?

Collateral damage?

I didn't know how to feel. But whatever I was feeling—it was too much.

I made it to my office without anyone seeing me.

Door shut. Lock turned.

And I stood there.

Just stood.

Arms braced against my desk. Head down.

Trying to breathe.

Trying not to scream.

I'd survived the breakup.

I'd even survived watching Ethan walk past me like I didn't exist.

But this?

This was another level of cruel.

The man who made me feel safe, wanted, *alive*—

The man who ruined me in the best way—

Was the father of the man who tore me apart.

And I had no one to blame but myself.

I didn't sit. I didn't cry.

I just stood there, staring at the floor, waiting for something inside me to stop spinning.

A knock.

I didn't answer.

The knock came again. Heavier.

Then his voice.

James.

"Lexi. Open the door."

I didn't.

The lock clicked.

Of course he had a key.

James stepped in, closing the door behind him. He didn't speak at first. Just looked at me—really looked.

"You've been crying," he said.

"Sharp observation," I muttered.

He came closer. Controlled. Purposeful.

"What the hell happened?"

I laughed, but there was no humour in it. "You really don't know."

His jaw flexed. "If I knew, I wouldn't be asking."

I turned to face him, arms crossed tightly. "You want to know what's wrong?"

"Yes," he snapped. "Before I lose my god damn mind trying to figure it out."

"Ethan," I said.

He stilled.

Like a statue caught mid-step.

"What about him?" His voice was quieter now. More dangerous.

I looked him dead in the eye.

"He's my ex."

The silence that followed wasn't empty.

It was thick. Unforgiving.

I watched it land. Watched the breath leave his body. Watched the wall go up behind his eyes like a steel door slamming shut.

"Say that again," he said, but his voice was dead now.

"I dated him," I said. "For a year. Until two months ago, when I walked in on him fucking someone else."

James stepped back.

One pace.

Two.

"No," he muttered. "No, no, no—fuck."

He ran a hand through his hair, pacing like the floor might open under him.

"I didn't know," he said, like it mattered. "I swear to god, I didn't know."

"I know you didn't," I said coldly. "You think I'd have touched you if I had?"

He looked up, wild-eyed. "You think I'd have *let you*?"

We stared at each other. Silence stretching like a wire about to snap.

"This is a disaster," he growled. "This is a fucking disaster."

My lip curled. "Thanks."

"Don't twist it," he snapped. "I didn't need this right now. I didn't plan this."

"No," I said. "You just walked into my life, wrecked my rules, ruined my body, and forgot to mention the one thing that could make me feel sick to my stomach every time I think about you."

His eyes darkened. "Watch your mouth."

"Or what?" I said, stepping toward him. "You'll make me forget again? Like in the conference room? Like on my desk? That's your move, right? Dominate until the truth disappears?"

He stared at me.

Chest rising. Breathing hard.

But he didn't deny it.

And I hated that part of me wanted him to touch me again anyway.

"You said you were dangerous," I whispered.

"I am," he said.

And for once, I believed it.

"You're the disaster," he added, low and hard.

The words hung in the air, bitter and electric.

But I didn't flinch. I smiled—tight, sharp. A mouth full of venom and pride.

"Coming from the man who blew up a one-night stand into a full-blown identity crisis," I said. "Please. You don't even get to call me that unless you learn how to take responsibility for something other than your ego."

He stepped closer.

"I took responsibility the second I walked into that locker room and looked my son in the eye."

"Yeah?" I scoffed. "That before or after you dropped your pants in the board room?"

His eyes darkened. Not anger. Something worse.

Possession.

"You're the one who let me in, *kotyonok*," he murmured.

"Don't call me that."

His mouth tilted into a smirk that wasn't kind.

"You liked it."

"You're delusional," I bit out.

"You're still wet for me," he said, voice like silk-wrapped sin.

My pulse spiked. My thighs clenched before I could stop them.

And he saw it.

Of course he did.

"You're sick," I whispered, but my voice broke on the word.

He leaned in—slow, deliberate, dangerous.

"Maybe," he said, eyes locked to mine. ''But you certainly liked it.''

And that ruined me.

Because he meant it.

And it was the one thing I couldn't afford to want.

15

Chapter 15

Lexi

He didn't slam the door.

Of course not. That would've required emotion. Expression.

James Volkov didn't explode—he *imploded.* Quiet. Controlled. Cold.

Like he hadn't just rearranged every nerve in my body and then left me standing in the wreckage.

So he walked out of my office.

And I stood there, heart in my throat, fists clenched, staring at a door that suddenly felt very final.

Five minutes later I was texting the only two people who could handle this level of psychological damage.

> *✦ WINE WITCHES ✎♥︎🍷 – Group chat*
> *Lexi: get to the house. now. emergency.*
> *Rachel: do I need to bring a shovel or tequila*
> *Maya: is this an "I committed a felony" emergency or a "he's hot but I regret it" emergency*

Lexi: both. and worse.

Rachel: ten minutes out. wearing sweatpants and judgment.

Maya: grabbing wine and cheese. emotionally un-available but ready to enable.

By the time they arrived, I was already in my softest hoodie, sitting on the couch with a blanket like it might protect me from my own life choices.

Rachel kicked the door shut with her foot and threw a bag of snacks on the counter like she was storming a battlefield. "Alright. What the hell happened. Give me the full dramatic breakdown or I swear I'll start guessing."

Maya followed with wine, looking suspiciously excited. "Did the hot coach finally say he loves you and now you're panicking? Because same."

I blinked at them. "No. It's worse."

Rachel cracked open a bottle. "Did he ghost you? Cheat on you? If so, I will *light him on fire.*"

I shook my head and whispered it before I could stop myself. "He's Ethan's dad."

Silence.

Maya blinked. "I'm sorry, did you just say—"

Rachel dropped the wine glass. It bounced on the carpet. "ETHAN *WILSON?!* THE DICKBAG CHEATER?!"

"YES," I shrieked. "YES, THAT ETHAN."

Rachel fell to her knees, full drama. "OH MY GOD. THIS IS THE BEST THING THAT HAS EVER HAPPENED."

Maya covered her mouth, eyes wide. "Lexi. Babe. You... accidentally banged your ex's dad."

I nodded, face buried in my hands. "Multiple times."

Rachel rolled onto her back, howling. "THIS IS BETTER THAN REVENGE. THIS IS COSMIC JUSTICE."

Maya poured me a drink like she was knighting me. "You didn't just sleep with a new man. You *slept your way up the Wilson family tree.* You legend."

I groaned. "It's not funny."

"It's hilarious," Rachel said, wiping tears from her eyes. "He cheated on you, and you responded by accidentally going full Greek tragedy and seducing *his father.* That's not just revenge. That's *biblical.*"

"I feel sick."

"You should feel powerful," Maya said. "Like some kind of petty forest witch. You've ascended."

Rachel raised her glass. "To Lexi. May your enemies never know peace, and may your sex life continue to terrify us all."

We drank.

And for the first time all day, I laughed.

16

Chapter 16

Lexi

The next few afternoons, I was back at the arena, fully caffeinated and attempting to forget I had ever had sex, emotions, or a social life outside of memes and rage texting. My goal? Content. Distraction. Professional excellence. Also, to survive a whole day without seeing Ethan's stupid face or collapsing into a hormonal puddle over his very off-limits father.

The media team had me wrangling a few of the guys for some pre-season content—aka, the chaos circus. Today's victims: Carter, Connor, Liam, and Eli. I prayed for strength.

I was setting up near the practice rink, clipboard in hand and TikTok drafts ready to go, when the group showed up like a walking personality test.

Carter was already shirtless, despite the 40-degree air conditioning. "Lex, what's the plan? Please tell me it involves me lip-syncing shirtless to something deeply inappropriate. The internet deserves this jawline."

"You're doing the trending dance challenge in a mascot

helmet," I said.

"Even better."

Connor arrived next, holding a tray of iced coffees and two muffins. "I didn't know what you needed, so I got snacks. Also, I love your hoodie. You doing okay? You recovering from a certain someone on the team?"

"Connor, you're too pure for this world."

"Tell my abs that," he said sweetly.

Liam appeared last, sliding in like he was about to cause a scene. He was wearing sunglasses indoors. "Lexi. Goddess. Boss witch. Content queen. Tell me what chaos you desire."

"I want the four of you to stop acting like you're auditioning for a dating show and just follow the script."

"So no sexy voiceovers in slow motion?"

"Liam."

He winked. "Just sayin'. We tested well with Gen Z."

Somewhere behind them, I spotted Ethan. Skating drills. Eyes down. Avoiding me like I was radioactive.

Good.

Carter leaned in, dropping his voice. "He hasn't said a word to about you at all. Been skating solo like he's punishing the ice since we all got back."

"Fine by me," I muttered.

Connor offered me the second muffin. "He should be punishing himself. And also, you should eat something that isn't vengeance."

"Is this banana?"

"With chocolate chips."

I blinked. "You're perfect."

"I know."

I started filming them one at a time. Carter hamming it up

with finger guns. Connor doing the dance too seriously, like he was auditioning for a musical. Liam attempting to do a dramatic reading of his own Instagram comments.

I laughed. For real. Genuinely.

This—the chaos, the banter, the boys who chose me when someone else didn't—this felt like healing.

Liam grabbed my phone halfway through and started vlogging. "Day three of being trapped with our emotional support media manager who may or may not have a god complex and honestly? We respect her for it."

Carter added, "We're not saying we'd die for her, but if she asked us to egg someone's car, we would ask whose."

Connor held up a banana muffin like a toast. "To Lexi. Queen of content. Breaker of hearts. Destroyer of cheating exes."

I felt my throat tighten. Just a little.

And then Liam added quietly, "You know we're Team Lexi, right? Always. Even though we love Ethan, he knows what he did was wrong."

I nodded. Couldn't speak. Didn't need to.

Because even with everything shattered, these idiots were helping me rebuild. outside of memes and rage texting. My goal? Content. Distraction. Professional excellence. Also, to survive a whole day without staring directly at James Volkov like he was the human equivalent of a forbidden snack.

Chapter 17

Lexi

The first home game of the season was HERE.

There was nothing like it—music pounding through the arena, lights dancing across the ice, and that thick, electric hum of anticipation. The kind of energy you could feel in your ribs. The kind of energy that turned full-grown adults into screaming lunatics over a rubber disc.

I stood just off the tunnel, clipboard in hand, headset in place, doing my best impression of someone who wasn't running on caffeine, adrenaline, and a long, long list of bad decisions. The team was already on the ice, warming up. The puck hadn't dropped yet, but the crowd was alive. And so were my nerves.

Connor caught my eye as he skated past, tapping his stick against the boards with a cocky grin.

"Lex! You see my new pads? I told you they were sexy."

"They're fine," I called back, smirking. "Try not to get scored on in them."

"Ouch." He clutched his chest. "You wound me."

Liam and Ryan followed behind him, tossing chirps back and forth like they were on a sitcom.

"Connor's just mad you said *his* gear was 'fine' but called Liam's new haircut 'game-changing,'" Ryan teased.

"That's because Liam's haircut doesn't let pucks in," I shot back.

Liam turned to grin at me. "You've got my number tonight, don't you?"

I raised my eyebrows. "On my back, yes. Don't let it go to your head."

The guys cracked up and skated off, leaving me with a half-smile and the sense that, for once, I might actually enjoy tonight.

Last season, I'd worn Ethan's jersey to almost every game. Hadn't even thought about it—just muscle memory, a habit carved from years of supporting someone I thought I loved. But now?

Now, I was cycling through every other number on the team like it was therapy.

Tonight was Liam.

Next week? Maybe Connor. Or Ryan. Or literally anyone whose idea of romance didn't involve betrayal and a backup dancer.

"Lex!"

I turned just as Rachel and Maya burst into the media row behind the bench, both wearing matching oversized jerseys like they were about to star in their own hype reel.

Rachel wore Connor's number, obviously—part crush, part brand loyalty.

Maya? Her jersey was blank. "Mystery. Intrigue. Power," she said when I asked. "Also I couldn't commit to a number because I like to keep my options open."

Classic Maya.

They leaned over the rail as I stepped up to the bench to check on one of the live-feed screens.

Rachel grinned like the devil in lipstick. "Soooooo... what are we thinking for next game? Ryan? That new rookie? Maybe Coach Daddy..."

"Don't."

Maya's eyes sparkled. "Oooh, now *there's* an idea. You already wore his mouth—why not the jersey?"

"Do not say that in front of the children," I hissed.

Rachel pointed dramatically. "I'm just saying, you could start a *trend*. Player jersey one game, Coach's the next. Real 'Who's wrecking Lexi this week?' energy."

I covered my face with my clipboard. "I will smother both of you with rally towels."

Maya leaned closer, voice lower now. "But seriously... he hasn't stopped watching you since you walked out here."

I didn't look. I didn't need to.

I could feel it.

From across the ice, across the noise, across the stadium full of chaos and adrenaline and expectations—I could feel James Volkov watching me like I was the only thing on the scoreboard.

My skin buzzed with it. My body remembered it.

Which was bad.

Very, very bad.

Because this was the season opener.

This was *my* job.

And I was standing in front of a packed arena with a man who'd bent me over my own desk three days ago and left me gasping his name.

Rachel nudged me. "Girl. He's *seething.*"

I dared a glance toward the bench.

James stood at the far end, arms crossed, headset on, jaw clenched. Completely unreadable to anyone else.

But I knew that look.

Possession. Frustration. Hunger.

I turned back to the girls, face neutral. "I am *not* wearing his jersey."

Rachel grinned. "I bet he wants you in just that and nothing else."

Maya held up her beer. "To the hottest PR scandal we're *almost* rooting for."

I rolled my eyes, heart pounding louder than the crowd.

The music swelled.

The lights dimmed.

And the team skated out.

Connor made a face at Rachel as he passed the glass. Liam winked at me. Ryan blew a kiss at some poor intern near the bench.

And Ethan?

He didn't look at me.

Didn't even glance.

But I saw the way his jaw tightened when he noticed whose number was on my back.

And I smiled.

Just a little.

Let the games begin.

* * *

The first period was electric.

Connor was in full brick-wall mode, making saves that had the whole arena roaring. Liam landed a beauty of a shot halfway through the period, and the celebration that followed was pure chaos—gloves in the air, stick raised, a dive into the boards like he was sliding into home base.

"That's what happens when I wear your number," I muttered under my breath, watching from the bench with a grin.

But it was Ethan who had everyone losing their minds.

He was everywhere. Fast, sharp, ruthless. Skating like he had something to prove—and maybe he did. Every pass was clean. Every play calculated. By the time he scored his second goal of the night, the arena was on its feet, deafening.

I didn't cheer.

But I didn't look away either.

He didn't glance at me when he skated past the bench. Didn't smirk. Didn't gloat. Just stared straight ahead like the goal was already forgotten.

Which somehow made it worse.

Rachel's voice popped up in my headset from the media booth. "You seeing this? Your ex is *feral* tonight."

"Shut up," I hissed.

"I mean, if that's how he played after being dumped, maybe we should break up the whole team. You want Connor next?"

"You're fired."

"Rude. But fair."

I muted her mic and leaned down to adjust the bench monitor. Just busywork. Something to do that didn't involve staring at the back of Ethan's jersey.

Which is, of course, when it happened.

A shadow fell over me. Heat.

I turned.

83

James.

Standing behind me.

Too close. Too casual. Pretending like he had a reason to be this near when he absolutely did not.

"What are you doing?" I asked, voice low.

He didn't answer. Just reached past me—unnecessarily—under the bench to grab one of the trainer clipboards.

His arm brushed mine.

"Seriously?" I hissed.

He didn't even blink. "Had to make sure the backup lines are updated."

"They're literally taped to the glass, Volkov."

He leaned in slightly, his voice low and meant just for me. "You think I don't notice what number you're wearing?"

My breath caught.

"I thought we agreed to be professional," I said.

He glanced down at my jersey—Liam's number printed bold across my back. His jaw tightened. "You think that number means anything?"

"It means he's not your son," I snapped.

Wrong move.

His eyes darkened. "Don't start something here unless you're ready to finish it somewhere else."

And then—he was gone.

Back to his post like he hadn't just made my entire rib cage feel like it was wrapped in barbed wire and tension.

Across the ice, Ethan lined up for a faceoff.

The puck dropped.

And just like that, the game pulled me back in.

By the end of the second, we were up 3-1. The fans were foaming at the mouth, the announcers were losing it, and I was clinging to the edge of the bench like it might keep me sane.

I didn't know what was worse—Ethan on fire, James smoldering, or the fact that I was smack in the middle of it all, wearing a jersey that didn't belong to either of them.

Maya texted me mid-period, even though she knew I wouldn't answer.

MAYA: *Coach Volkov looks like he's trying not to set the entire arena on fire with his eyes.*

MAYA: *Also Ethan is playing like he's possessed. What's in the water over there???*

MAYA: *Did you sleep with BOTH of them again??!?!?*

I shoved my phone in my pocket and tried to breathe.

Third period was coming.

And I had a bad feeling the ice wasn't the only place things were about to get messy.

* * *

The third period started fast.

The kind of fast that made your chest tighten and your pulse race—even from the sidelines.

We were up by two, but the other team was hungry. Desperate. Throwing checks like it was the playoffs, not game one. The crowd was roaring. That kind of energy that buzzed in your bones.

Connor was on fire in net—fast glove, zero hesitation. Liam had an assist and was skating like he had rockets strapped to his skates. Ryan was chirping everyone like it was a personal hobby.

And Ethan...

Ethan was locked in.

Too locked in.

I felt his stare before I saw it—burning a hole into the bench, into me.

At the Liam jersey I was wearing.

It was just a tradition. Nothing serious. My way of supporting the team without wearing Ethan's number ever again. I told myself it wasn't a big deal.

But to him?

Oh, it was nuclear.

The puck flew into the corner, and both Ethan and Liam chased it down. They hit the boards hard, shoulder to shoulder—until Ethan threw a deliberate shove.

And then?

All hell broke loose.

The gloves hit the ice. Fists followed.

The arena exploded around them, the crowd on their feet, screaming. But the fight wasn't for show. It wasn't for the cameras.

It was real.

"You're supposed to be my *best friend*!" Ethan roared, fist catching Liam's shoulder as the refs blew whistles from all angles. "Why the fuck is she wearing your number?"

"She's not yours anymore!" Liam fired back, slamming Ethan into the glass with so much force it rattled. "You don't get to be pissed when you're the one who broke her! She's our friend too!"

Ethan lunged again. "You think I don't know what this is? You've been waiting for me to mess up. To slide in the second

I was gone—"

Liam shoved him back hard. "Don't flatter yourself. This isn't about *me* wanting her—it's about *you* treating her like she was nothing. And now you're mad she finally figured it out?"

"Don't pretend this is about loyalty," Ethan hissed, red-faced, blood already trickling from a split lip. "You were *always* looking for an excuse."

Liam snapped. "Yeah? Well now I've got one."

The refs surged between them, finally dragging them apart like they were wild animals on the edge of snapping teeth.

"You don't get to act like the victim," Liam growled, still trying to break free. "You cheated. You *destroyed* her. And now you want to play jealous ex because someone actually gives a shit?"

Ethan didn't respond.

Didn't even look at me—yet.

But when he did, when our eyes locked from across the ice, something twisted in his face.

Not rage.

Not pride.

Just guilt.

Like maybe he finally saw what he'd done.

But I didn't have it in me to offer him comfort. Or forgiveness.

Not anymore.

Because he'd had every chance to make things right.

And he'd waited until it was too late.

The players were pulled apart. Penalties were shouted. The crowd roared for blood like it was playoff season.

But all I could hear was my heartbeat.

All I could feel was James's eyes on me from the bench.

He hadn't said a word. Hadn't reacted.

Just stood there—stoic, ice cold, arms crossed—watching the boy he used to call son unravel in front of an entire arena.

And me?

I just stood frozen in the tension of it all.

Caught between a past I didn't want and a future I wasn't ready for.

And the war between them had only just begun.

18

Chapter 18

Lexi

The win didn't feel real until the final horn blasted through the arena.

The crowd roared. Players slammed gloves into backs. The bench emptied like a flood, helmets flying and adrenaline taking over. Our boys skated straight into each other like a victory pile-up was just as necessary as the final buzzer.

Despite the fight in the third period—despite the tension and bruised egos—we'd done it. Game one: ours.

Rachel and Maya were screaming next to me like they'd personally scored every goal. "Did you see Liam?" Maya shrieked, shaking my arm. "Like, okay, I know he's emotionally stunted and allergic to socks, but I want to build a church in his honour."

"I want to build a liquor fountain," Rachel countered. "And pour it directly into our mouths at the club tonight. Speaking of—Connor said they got us all VIP."

I blinked. "Since when?"

Rachel grinned. "Since Coach Daddy apparently knows people."

Right.

James.

I hadn't seen him since the fight broke out. I'd tried not to *look* for him. But that didn't mean I hadn't *felt* him—on the bench, eyes cutting through me like a blade made of fire and tension and every bad decision I wasn't done making.

We didn't speak after the game. I didn't even catch his eye as I followed the team and staff out of the arena and into the city's velvet nightlife.

But I felt it.

That storm.

Him.

* * *

The club was pulsing—low lights, loud music, and the kind of bass that felt like it lived in your bones. VIP wristbands got us past the crowd and up to the mezzanine, where bottle service and velvet ropes made us feel untouchable.

Connor was already two drinks in, shirt half unbuttoned like he'd just wandered out of a cologne ad. Ryan was holding court near the booth, retelling every dramatic second of the game like he hadn't just lived it. Liam was beside me, loose and grinning, his energy calmer now, but his arm kept brushing mine protectively—like he was still on edge after the fight.

Rachel and Maya were dancing like they were on a mission to ruin at least three men's lives before midnight.

It felt *good.*

Like I had space again. Like I could breathe.

Until Ethan showed up.

Late. Alone. Sober.

He moved through the club like someone walking into his own funeral—shoulders stiff, eyes hollow, dressed like he might vanish if I blinked.

Then he found me.

Near the bar. Drink in hand. Guard up.

"Can we talk?"

I didn't answer right away. Just looked at him. Looked at the man I used to fight for. And the man who stopped fighting for me.

"Please," he added.

There was no swagger this time. Just something frayed. Something fragile.

So I nodded. Not out of forgiveness. Just to finally hear what he had the nerve to say.

We stepped into the hallway by the bathrooms. Harsh lighting. Cold tile. The kind of place you go to fall apart without witnesses.

"I'm sorry," he said.

I blinked. "You practiced that line in the mirror, or are you hoping I'm drunk enough to believe it?"

He winced. "I deserve that."

"You deserve a lot worse."

He nodded. Hands shoved deep into his pockets like he didn't trust himself not to reach for me.

"I shouldn't have said what I said. At practice. About Liam. About you."

I tilted my head. "You mean the part where you embarrassed yourself in front of the team because I was wearing someone else's number?"

"I was jealous," he admitted. "Not of Liam. Of you. Of how happy you looked. How light. I hadn't seen you like that in a long time."

I laughed. Bitter. Sharp. "Yeah, well, you didn't exactly give me a lot of reasons to feel light."

He looked down. "I didn't cheat because I stopped loving you."

"Oh, cool. So you betrayed me while still loving me. What a *comfort*."

"I didn't come here to justify it," he said, and for once, he looked like he meant it. "I just wanted you to know I see it now. What I did. What it cost."

"Do you?" I asked. "Do you really get what it felt like? To walk in and see you with them—*laughing, enjoying your self like that*—like I'd never even existed?"

He closed his eyes. Took a breath like he was trying to hold himself together.

"Yes," he said quietly. "Because I was trying, too. I just didn't know how to tell you that everything felt wrong, even when you were doing everything right."

He took another breath, slower this time, like it hurt to admit it.

"I loved you," he said, voice cracking. "I really did."

"I know," I whispered. Because I did. That was never the question.

He gave a soft, broken laugh. "And maybe that's the worst part. That I could love you that much and still ruin it. Still not be what you needed. Maybe we were never meant to work."

And there it was.

The sentence that ended it all. Not with hate. Not with blame. But with truth. The kind that sticks to your ribs long after it's spoken.

I blinked back the sting behind my eyes.

"I'm glad you said it," I told him. "But that doesn't mean I forgive you."

"I don't expect you to."

"Good." I paused. "Because I'm not sure I ever will."

He nodded. Said nothing. Because there was nothing left to say. He left to go to were the others were stood.

I turned to walk outside to get some air—

And stopped.

Because James was there.

By the railing. Watching. Still. Dark.

His jaw was tight. His posture carved from tension. One of the assistant coaches stood beside him, talking—completely ignored.

Because his eyes were locked on me.

And I couldn't tell if he looked more like he wanted to walk away...

Or come closer.

19

Chapter 19

James

Of course she looked like sin wrapped in gold.

Of course every man in that club had his eyes on her like she was free to take.

And of course, Ethan had gotten to her first.

I watched it all—from the balcony, from the crowd, from the damn shadows like a man who had no right but every reason to claim her.

And I *had* claimed her.

But it still wasn't enough.

She laughed like she hadn't shattered in my arms. Smiled like she didn't ache the same way I did.

She didn't see me at first.

Too busy laughing with her friends, dancing like she didn't belong to anyone—like she hadn't moaned my name just days ago.

But I saw *him*—Ethan—touching her shoulder. Leaning in too close. Smiling like he deserved a second chance.

And that's when the switch flipped. I lost control of right and wrong.

I moved from the shadows, slow and lethal. No words. No warning.

She turned, and before she could even speak, I grabbed her wrist and pulled.

Sharp inhale. Stumbling heels. Confused eyes.

She didn't protest.

Didn't ask where I was taking her.

Because she already *knew*.

Down the hallway. Past the velvet ropes. Through the door no one else dared use.

I shoved it open, dragged her inside, and slammed it behind us.

So when I pulled her into my office—*my fucking territory*—I didn't wait.

I slammed the door and locked it behind us.

She whirled on me, breath already ragged. "You can't keep doing this—"

I crossed the space in two strides, grabbing her by the waist and hauling her against me. My mouth found hers before she could finish. I didn't kiss her. I consumed her. Possessive. Hard. Furious.

"You think I didn't see him touching you?" I growled against her lips. "Think I didn't see every man in that club looking at what's *mine*?"

Her breath caught. "James—"

"No. Not tonight, *kotyonok*." My hand slid up her thigh, dragging that tiny gold dress with it. "Tonight, I remind you who you belong to."

She gasped as I spun her, pressing her to the wall—palms

flat, legs trembling.

"I don't share," I whispered against her ear, voice all smoke and heat. "I don't ask."

Then I dropped to my knees.

Not with reverence.

With hunger.

And I lost myself with her. Lost every ounce of control I had left.

Her back slammed into the wall as I shoved her there, hard enough to knock the breath from her lungs. I grabbed her thighs, ripped her legs apart like I had a goddamn right to. Her panties? I didn't move them aside—I *tore* them. One violent tug. Gone.

She gasped, and I looked up at her, eyes blazing.

"Don't fucking look at me like that unless you want to be broken."

Her breath caught. Her pupils were blown, lips parted, chest heaving like she couldn't breathe unless I was the one allowing it.

So I gave her air the only way I knew how—

I ate her like she was mine.

Not slow. Not soft.

I went in hard—tongue deep, mouth devouring, jaw locked. I wasn't trying to build her up. I was trying to drag her under.

She cried out, grabbed my hair, tried to control the rhythm.

I growled. Bit her thigh. Hard.

She whimpered—and *gushed.*

"You want control?" I snarled against her. "Then get on top. Otherwise—shut up and take what I give you."

I sucked her clit so hard she buckled. She tried to close her legs—I grabbed her hips and *slammed* her back against the wall.

Then my hand went to her throat.

I gripped it—not choking, not soft. Enough to hold. To dominate.

Her entire body shuddered. She was drenched.

"Of course that turns you on," I muttered. "You don't want love. You want to be ruined."

She nodded. Frantic. No shame. Just need.

So I made her regret wanting me.

Two fingers shoved inside her. Rough. Crooked just right to make her scream.

I fucked her with them while I sucked her clit—relentless, brutal, no reprieve.

She was soaked. *Shaking.* Her thighs trembled, her cries growing high and tight, panic-laced pleasure.

"You gonna come on my fucking face?" I growled. "Do it. Let them hear you."

And she did.

Loud. Guttural.

Her whole body shattered—legs giving out, hands slapping the wall behind her for balance, throat under my palm as I held her together while she broke.

She didn't just come.

She *detonated.*

When she collapsed forward, gasping, ruined, I didn't catch her gently.

I grabbed her by the waist and kissed her like I was claiming territory.

And when she finally looked at me again—red-faced, trembling, wild—I smiled.

"Soft love isn't in your blood."

"You need something that hurts."

"And I'm the one who gives it to you."

Fuck—*I wasn't supposed to want this.*

I came here to fix things. To make it right with Ethan. To earn back a son who had every reason to shut me out.

Not to take the one girl who could wreck us both.

Not to crave her like a curse I *chose.*

I should've walked away the second I found out. Should've shut this down. Should've let her go—because she wasn't mine to want.

But I did want her.

I wanted her like sin. Like oxygen. Like absolution I didn't deserve.

And hating myself for it didn't make it stop.

I didn't come here to destroy Ethan. But this? *This would destroy him.*

And still—my hands were on her. My mouth was already searching for the places that made her fall apart. My need had already drowned my conscience.

Because the second I touched her, I knew I was already past the point of no return.

I didn't want to hurt my son.

But I couldn't stop hurting him.

And maybe that made me a monster.

But the worst part?

I'd do it again.

20

Chapter 20

Lexi

I could still feel him on my skin.

His mouth.

His hands.

His voice, low and brutal and burning in my ear like it had been branded there.

I didn't remember leaving his office—only the sharp click of the door behind me and the way my legs had to relearn how to work. My body was humming. My heart? Still somewhere back on that desk, bleeding and wrecked.

The club hit me like a slap. Lights. Music. People. It was too loud, too bright, too *normal*.

I took a shaky breath and adjusted my dress, praying to the gods of fabric and dignity that I didn't look as absolutely ravaged as I felt. But the second I stepped back into the VIP area, Rachel and Maya locked eyes with me—and it was *over*.

Rachel's brows shot up so high they nearly launched off her face. Maya's mouth curved into a knowing, slightly evil smile.

I tried to dodge. Sit. Breathe. Pretend I'd just gotten lost on the way to the bathroom and not been torn apart by the man I wasn't supposed to want.

"Hey!" Liam called, spotting me. "There she is!"

Connor nudged a drink into my hand like I hadn't just committed a very intense series of mistakes.

"You okay?" he asked, easygoing grin on his face.

"Yeah," I lied. "Totally. Great. So great."

"You look..." Ryan squinted. "Flushed."

"Dancing," I said too fast. "I was dancing."

Rachel choked on her drink.

Maya elbowed her. "You should've seen the way she moved out there. Practically... *glowing.*"

I shot them both a murderous look.

But it didn't matter—because now the guys were crowding in, pulling me into the circle, drinks clinking and jokes flying, the energy shifting into something looser, louder, easier.

I sat. I smiled. I laughed at a dumb story about Tanner losing a bet and having to wear a glittery crop top to practice.

But under it all?

I could still feel him.

Between my legs.

On my lips.

In every broken breath I tried to hide.

And across the room, behind the glass wall of the VIP lounge, James Volkov was watching.

Eyes dark. Arms folded.

Like he hadn't just ruined me.

Like he was already planning how to do it again.

It was almost laughable, how normal everything looked.

Liam was deep in conversation with Maya, flailing dramatically about some rookie disaster that had apparently involved Gatorade, a jockstrap, and one deeply unfortunate Instagram Live. Ryan was holding court near the bar, retelling a game highlight like it was a Greek myth and he was the chosen one.

And me?

I was just... trying to breathe.

My dress was wrinkled from where James had gripped it. My thighs still trembled with the ghost of him. And my lipstick? Long gone. Eaten away by a man who'd tasted me like a fucking addiction.

I didn't even have time to fix it before Rachel spotted me.

Her eyes flicked over my face, then my body, and narrowed just slightly.

But—bless her chaotic, gorgeous soul—she didn't say a word. Just handed me a drink and raised a brow like we'd circle back later for the post-mortem.

I took it. Sipped like it was oxygen.

And then I saw them.

Rachel, turning away, laughing. And Connor—towering, tattooed, and entirely unfair—watching her like she was the only thing in the room worth looking at. His jaw was sharp, the kind that could cut glass or egos, and his shirt clung in all the right places, sleeves rolled to reveal ink that looked far too good for someone who also had reflexes fast enough to deflect slapshots.

He leaned in, said something low in her ear.

Rachel grinned, slow and wicked. "Oh, sweetheart. You couldn't handle me."

Connor smirked. "Babe, I block pucks with my face for fun. You think I'm scared of a redhead with eyeliner and attitude?"

"I'm not just a redhead," she said, turning fully toward him now. "I'm a goddamn personality trait."

"Good," he said, stepping closer. "I like a challenge."

The air around them practically *snapped*. People danced inches away, oblivious. But right there—in that corner of the VIP lounge—it was fire and danger and flirtation so sharp it could draw blood.

I blinked. Looked away. My heart was already doing gymnastics and I didn't need to be collateral damage in whatever sexual power struggle was about to unfold over the club's complimentary bottle service.

But I couldn't help it—my eyes drifted back.

Rachel had her hand on his chest now, like she was daring him to move. And Connor? He didn't move. Didn't flinch. Just stared down at her like she was both the battle and the reward.

"I'm not one of your fangirls," she said.

"I know," he said. "You're worse."

And somehow, they both looked like they were enjoying every second of it.

I turned back to my drink, brain already filing away this moment as something we'd all be talking about by sunrise.

And maybe, just for a second, the knot in my chest loosened.

Because if they could still laugh, still flirt, still find something electric in the middle of all the mess...

Maybe I wasn't completely doomed after all.

* * *

By the time we made it into the Uber, I was still vibrating.

Not metaphorically. *Literally.* My thighs were pressed together like I was afraid the memory of James might crawl out and confess to the driver.

I slid into the middle seat, which in retrospect was a terrible choice—boxed in by two women who'd seen the look on my face the moment I walked back into that club.

Maya shut the door behind her and immediately turned, eyes blazing. "Start talking."

Rachel raised a hand like she was in court. "Seconded."

I blinked. "We're barely two blocks away."

"Exactly," Maya said. "You've had one minute to gather your thoughts. Time's up."

"Guys—"

Rachel leaned in, grinning like the gremlin she was. "Don't make me guess. I *will* guess. And I've been drinking, so my guesses will involve costumes."

"You disappeared for like half an hour," Maya said. "Then came back looking like you'd been exorcised via orgasm. We're not stupid."

"I'm not doing this in front of the Uber driver," I hissed, glancing toward the front seat.

He raised a hand without looking back. "Don't worry. I'm wearing noise-canceling AirPods and emotionally detached from all of you."

"See?" Maya beamed. "We're safe."

I groaned and dropped my head into my hands.

Rachel poked my arm. "Did he touch you again?"

Maya: "Did he *look* at you like he was going to devour you again?"

Rachel: "Did he *devour* you again?!"

My voice came out a strangled whisper. "It was his office."

Maya gasped so dramatically the driver actually flinched. "The office?!"

103

"Whose office?!" Rachel demanded.

"*His* office," I hissed. "He *owns* the club."

The car went silent for a second.

And then both of them shrieked like we'd just hit a raccoon.

Rachel clutched her chest. "Oh my GOD, you let him ravish you in a room he *owns*? That's—hold on, I need to text someone about this and I don't even know who."

Maya was already halfway into composing a tweet she would never post. "*Girl gets destroyed by mystery coach in luxury sex lair he owns. Film at 11.*"

"You are not helping," I groaned.

"No, but we *are* thrilled," Rachel said.

"Also you're glowing again," Maya added. "Which I hate."

"I don't know what I'm doing," I muttered.

Rachel's voice softened slightly. "We know. But it's okay. He's hot and you're spiraling and we'll fix it with breakfast carbs and trauma-bonding."

Maya leaned her head on my shoulder. "Besides, at least you're not the *second* most chaotic person tonight."

I blinked. "What are you—"

They both turned to look at Rachel.

Rachel scowled. "No."

Maya grinned. "Yes."

"Absolutely not."

"Confess, witch," I said, pointing dramatically. "I saw you and Connor. You guys were practically a music video."

Rachel crossed her arms. "It was flirting. That's all."

"Flirting that looked like it needed a warning label," Maya said. "Or a cold shower."

Rachel rolled her eyes. "It's not like that. We just... banter."

"You banter with your mouth half an inch from his chest

tattoo?" I asked.

"He's tall!" she snapped. "I was looking *up*! And anyway, he's not my type."

Maya smirked. "Oh, you mean emotionally available, kind, built like a Greek statue, and clearly obsessed with you?"

"Exactly," Rachel said, then paused. "Wait—"

I laughed so hard I nearly choked.

Rachel groaned and slumped into her seat. "I hate you both."

Maya raised her phone like a toast. "To the witches of bad decisions."

I raised mine. "And the chaos we rode in on."

Rachel muttered, "I should've taken my own Uber."

And still, she smiled.

Even in the mess of everything—we had each other. And right now, that was enough.

21

Chapter 21

James

First away game of the season. The kind of milestone that should've had my full focus. New city. First impressions. Tensions high. Every detail mattered—from logistics to line changes. Eyes on me. Pressure everywhere.

And yet.

All I could think about was her.

It had been a week since the night in my office at the club. A week since I'd dropped to my knees and tasted her like she was salvation and sin wrapped into one devastating package. A week of pretending I was still in control.

Spoiler: I wasn't.

That night had embedded itself in my skull, clawed into my skin. It haunted me in quiet moments. In the locker room. In the dark. In dreams that left me hard and furious and alone.

The locker room before departure was loud. Borderline feral. Bags slammed. Players shouting over one another. Liam tried to climb through the luggage hold to "find his lucky stick."

Someone had duct-taped Ryan's skates together. It was chaos.

I didn't speak. I didn't need to. They respected silence more than shouting.

I moved through the madness with a mask of control—but the truth? I was two seconds from unraveling.

Because I saw her.

Across the tarmac, Lexi moved through the staff like a general in heels. Clipboard balanced against her chest. Coffee gripped like it owed her something. Ponytail bouncing, headphones in. Efficient. Commanding. Effortlessly fucking beautiful.

And completely off-limits.

She didn't see me at first. But when she did, she smiled—soft, barely there. Just enough to destroy me.

I looked away before I did something stupid. Like walk across the tarmac and remind her exactly how she sounded coming on my mouth.

I boarded the plane early. Picked a seat near the front. Away from the players. Away from temptation. Safe.

And then—

"Anyone sitting here?"

My spine snapped straight. Her voice. Low. Soft. Like it was meant for me alone.

I didn't look at her. Couldn't.

"Probably a player," I muttered.

"So... no?"

I didn't answer. That was all she needed.

She sat.

And just like that, the space shrank.

Because I'd spent the last week avoiding her like it was my job. Like if I kept my distance, I could somehow rewrite the past month.

I told myself it was for Ethan. That if I kept things clean, if I stopped acting like a fucking teenager with a god complex, I could earn his trust. Be the father I never got the chance to be.

But Lexi made that impossible. Every time she was near, every time her voice curled into my gut like smoke—I forgot. Forgot why I was here. Forgot who I was supposed to be.

Forgot I was trying to do the right thing.

And the worst part? I didn't want to remember.

She shifted in the seat beside me. Crossed her legs like a weapon.

"You planning to ignore me the whole trip or just until we take off?" she asked, voice sweet but sharp underneath.

I clenched my jaw. Said nothing.

"Because I can move," she added, coolly. "If I'm too much of a distraction for your holy redemption arc."

I turned, eyes locking on hers. Her expression was unreadable. But her pupils were wide. Her throat worked like she was swallowing something down.

"You think this is easy for me?" I said, low. "You think I'm enjoying pretending you don't exist?"

"Then stop pretending," she shot back.

I leaned in slightly, jaw tight. "If I stop now, I won't be able to. Stop. At all."

Her lips parted.

"So what, you're some kind of martyr now?" she bit out. "Sacrificing me for the greater good? For Ethan's peace of mind?"

I narrowed my eyes. "Don't twist this. You know damn well why I'm trying. You know damn well what touching you will cost me."

"You think you're protecting him, but maybe you're just afraid. Afraid of what you feel. Afraid of what you'd do if you let yourself have what you want. Maybe he will get over it."

I inhaled through my nose. Slow. Controlled. Barely.

"You already wrecked me, Lexi," I said quietly. "But if I touch you again, there's no coming back. Not for me. Not for you. And not for him."

Her eyes flickered.

"Good," she whispered. "Because I'm done pretending I didn't want to be wrecked."

Silence. The kind that crackled between us.

She was killing me.

Two hours of proximity. Two hours of her thigh brushing mine, her perfume curling through my bloodstream like smoke. Two hours of pretending I wasn't hard just from the sound of her breathing. From the memory of her coming undone on my tongue. From the way she kept shifting like she wanted me to snap.

"Comfortable?" I asked, still staring out the window like I could will myself somewhere else. Somewhere safer. Somewhere without her.

"Extremely," she said sweetly.

Fucking menace.

"Lexi."

"I know," she said, voice dipping lower. "We're not doing anything. I'm just sitting here."

Her tone was soft. Innocent. It made me want to ruin her.

She crossed her legs slowly. Deliberate. One thigh dragging over the other like a goddamn sin. My pulse kicked. My jaw locked. I wanted to grab her under this tray table and show her what real consequences felt like.

"You know he's in the back, right?" she murmured. "Middle row. Hoodie pulled over his head. Asleep already."

Ethan.

As if I could forget.

I nodded once. "Doesn't change anything."

"No," she said. "But it makes it easier to breathe."

I turned then. Just enough to catch the smirk tugging at her lips. The glint in her eyes. Like she liked knowing what she did to me. Like she liked watching me suffer.

"You like pushing me, don't you?" I asked, voice darker now.

She tilted her head. Lashes fluttering. "You make it so easy."

Jesus fucking Christ.

I turned back toward the window, fist clenched in my lap so hard my knuckles popped.

"Your in-flight entertainment plan?" she asked. "Angry brooding? Or judging people for ordering tomato juice?"

"Silently judging you."

She laughed under her breath. Low. Warm. It coiled in my gut and tightened like a snare. I wanted to kiss her just to shut her up. To hear that sound again against my mouth.

She shifted in her seat, her knee brushing mine. I didn't move.

She leaned closer. Voice a whisper now, dripping with heat. "You know, if you keep glaring at the seat in front of you like that, it's going to file a restraining order."

"I'm just trying not to look at you."

"Why?"

I turned. Locked eyes with her.

"Because if I do," I said quietly, "I'm going to forget where we are. Who we are. And I'll touch you. Right here. In front of everyone."

Her lips parted. Her eyes didn't waver.

"What if I want you to?" she whispered.

I didn't answer. I couldn't. My entire body was steel and fire and barely leashed hunger.

"You're scared," she said. "But not of getting caught. You're scared of how much you want me. Scared you'll lose control. Scared it won't be enough."

I leaned in until my mouth hovered next to her ear.

"If I lose control," I whispered, voice lethal, "you won't be able to walk off this plane without bruises."

She shivered. Smiled.

"Then maybe I'll stop trying to behave."

I exhaled hard. Turned away. My fists clenched, cock hard, jaw aching.

She closed her eyes. Tilted her head just slightly toward my shoulder.

Not touching me. But close enough I could feel her.

And I fucking liked it.

Because I wasn't just close to snapping. I wanted to snap. On her. For her. And she knew it.

When we landed, I was wrecked.

Lexi snapped back into work mode like she hadn't spent two hours torturing me with every breath. Clipboard out. Voice sharp. Eyes cool. Every part of her a perfect, pristine lie.

But I'd seen underneath. And I couldn't unsee it.

The bus ride to the hotel was loud. Jokes flying. Guys buzzing with travel adrenaline and anticipation.

Lexi sat three rows back, on the left. Laughing at something Liam said. Her head tilted back, her throat exposed. That sound? That fucking sound cut through me like a blade made of honey.

I stared out the window, fists clenched on my knees. I didn't turn around.

But I listened to her like it was oxygen. Like her voice was the only thing anchoring me to this goddamn reality.

At the hotel, staff filtered off first.

I stepped out. Pulled my jacket tighter. Tried to remember who I was supposed to be. Tried to find the man who wasn't on the edge of breaking.

And then I saw her.

At the check-in desk. Calm. Confident. Dangerous.

Our eyes met.

Fuck.

She held out a keycard. "You're on the top floor," she said, slipping it into my hand.

Her fingers brushed mine.

Intentional or not, I didn't give a shit.

"Convenient," I muttered.

"For what?" she asked, voice too smooth. Like she already knew the answer.

I looked at her. Let her see it—everything I was barely containing.

"You think I'm going to sneak up there later?"

"I think I'm not strong enough to stop you if you try."

Her breath caught. Her eyes flicked to my mouth. Her lips parted just slightly, like she could already feel me on her skin.

"That's not a no," she whispered.

I stepped closer. Just enough to make her inhale sharply.

"Don't test me, kotyonok," I said, voice low, dangerous. "You won't win."

She blinked, but didn't back down. Goosebumps rose along her collarbone. And her pupils—they were blown wide with want.

She liked it. She liked me like this. On edge. Unstable.

"Maybe I'm not trying to win," she said, barely audible. "Maybe I want to see what happens when you lose."

God. Fucking. Damn her.

"Coach?" a rookie called from the side. "Rooms are sorted. We're hitting the lounge after dinner."

I stepped back. Just a hair. Enough to look functional. Normal.

"Got it," I said. Voice steady. Expression neutral.

Mask back in place.

But as I walked away, every step felt like it was on borrowed time. Like my composure was glass—and she was already holding the hammer.

I wasn't strong. I wasn't composed.

I was a man held together by lies, pressure, and the taste of her still on my tongue.

And one more look from Lexi was all it would take to turn me into something unrecognizable.

Something that didn't give a damn who got hurt—as long as he got her.

22

Chapter 22

James

I didn't go to dinner.

Couldn't.

Not when I knew I'd spend the whole night staring across the table at her—Lexi—and pretending I wasn't thinking about her mouth, her moan, the way she looked when she... Jesus I need to get a grip.

So I stayed in.

Room service. Black coffee. A strategy doc open on my laptop like it could save me from my own lack of discipline.

It didn't.

The room was too quiet. Too clean. The air felt thick. Like it knew what I wanted. Like it was daring me to crack.

I'd stripped down to a T-shirt and sweats, trying to breathe past the ache in my chest. In my blood. Lower.

I glanced at the clock.

11:43 p.m.

Team should be in their rooms. Lights out. No distractions.

Except the one I couldn't stop thinking about.

Lexi.

Her voice. Her smirk. The press of her thigh against mine. The way she'd leaned in at check-in, breath hitching when I said her name like a warning and a promise.

I leaned back. Stared at the ceiling. Tried to force logic into my blood.

You've already crossed the line. You already touched what wasn't yours. You said it was a one-time thing.

I rubbed both hands down my face.

Weeks and she hadn't left my head. Not once. Not even in sleep.

And that look she gave me before I walked away?

She knew.

She knew I was one step from breaking.

And God help me, I wanted her to push me off the edge.

Then— Knock. Knock.

Two soft taps. Barely a warning. Just enough to shatter the thin thread holding my control together.

I opened the door.

And there she was.

Lexi. Hoodie. Bare legs. That mouth made for sin and war. Her eyes? Pure fucking challenge. Like she already knew I wasn't going to say no. Like she'd come here to finish what we both swore we wouldn't start again.

"Can't sleep?" I asked, voice flat. Rough. Tense.

She shrugged, one shoulder rising like she couldn't be bothered. "Didn't try very hard."

Jesus Christ.

I stepped back. Didn't invite her in. She came anyway.

115

Walked in slow, casual, like she owned the space. Like she owned *me.*

I shut the door with a hard click. Leaned against it. Arms crossed. Trying like hell not to grab her, throw her on the bed, and fuck the defiance right off her face.

"You're pushing your luck," I warned.

She turned. That look on her face—smug, daring, sweet enough to rot teeth. But her eyes? Her eyes were wicked.

"Thought you liked it when I pushed you."

My jaw clenched so tight it ached. My fingers flexed at my sides.

"I'm trying to be better," I said. Low. Dangerous. Each word pulled from somewhere just shy of breaking. "Trying not to make this worse."

She took a step forward, slow and taunting. Eyes locked on mine. No fear. No hesitation.

"Are you?"

Her voice was soft. But sharp enough to draw blood. A whisper wrapped in barbed wire.

I stepped toward her. Each step deliberate. Measured. Like I didn't want to tear through her, but wanted her to know I *could.*

She didn't move. Didn't blink.

"You know exactly what you're doing," I said, stopping just inches from her. My voice a threat. My pulse a war drum. "And you still came here."

She tilted her head, lips twitching like a knife being unsheathed.

"Maybe I needed reminding."

My hands curled into fists, knuckles aching to leave marks.

"Reminding of what?"

Her smile widened. Dark. Gleaming. Unrepentant.

"Of what you do to me."

That was it.

That was the second I stopped pretending.

I grabbed her by the waist and *slammed* her back against the wall. Hard. Not cruel—but no gentleness, no apology. I lifted her like she was weightless. Mine. She gasped, but didn't pull away. Didn't resist.

My mouth crashed into hers, devouring the sound. I bit down on her bottom lip until she whimpered—then she bit me back, sharp and possessive.

Good.

Because I wasn't here to be sweet. I was here to *wreck* her.

"You walk in here like you own me," I growled into her mouth, "and I let you. But don't mistake that for mercy."

She grinned, breath shaky against my jaw.

"Wouldn't dream of it."

I wrapped a hand around her throat—not choking, just holding. Owning. Her eyes blew wide. Her thighs tightened around my waist like instinct.

"You want ruin, baby?" I whispered, dark and ragged. "You came to the right fucking place."

I spun her around, fast. Bent her over the bed.

Her palms hit the mattress with a thud, legs parting instinctively.

I yanked the hoodie up over her back, exposing smooth skin and soft curves. No panties.

Of course not.

"You came to my room like this?" I growled. "No panties? Just attitude and nerve?"

She turned her head to look at me over her shoulder, hair falling in her face. "Knew you'd take care of it."

Oh, I will.

I brought my hand down across her ass, starting soft.

She yelped, breath catching.

"You want to be a brat?" *Smack, a little bit harder.*

"Come in here like you own me?" *Smack.*

"Say stupid shit like that?"

Smack. Hard.

She gasped, moaning now, breath turning shaky. Her ass flushed under my hand, red and hot and perfect.

I leaned in close, my mouth brushing her ear. "You want punishment, kotyonok? You just earned it."

She whimpered.

And I loved it.

I spanked her again, harder this time—then ran my fingers between her legs, dragging them through the slick heat waiting for me.

"So wet," I muttered. "All that attitude and you're dripping for me."

She moaned, body trembling.

I dropped to my knees behind her.

"Let's see how many times I can make you come before you learn some respect."

And then I *devoured* her.

Tongue deep, fingers tight around her thighs, holding her in place while she squirmed and screamed and came so hard she sobbed my name into the sheets.

I didn't stop.

Not until her legs gave out.

Not until her whole body was shaking.

I stood, breathing hard, and pulled her up by the waist. Turned her. Lifted her. Dropped her onto the center of the bed like she was mine.

"You think this is over?" I muttered, dragging my shirt off.

Lexi—wrecked, flushed, eyes dark with need—shook her head.

"Good."

I crawled over her.

Took her wrists.

Pinned them above her head.

"Tell me what you want."

Her voice was a whisper now. "I want *you*."

I didn't hesitate.

I thrust into her hard, burying myself to the hilt in one brutal motion.

She cried out, back arching, every nerve in her body catching fire under mine.

"Mine," I growled. "Say it."

"I'm yours," she gasped. "God, James—please—"

I fucked her deep, rough, rhythm steady and punishing. Her body moved with mine like she'd been made for this. For *me*.

"Ты моя. Только моя," I whispered, low and fierce.

(You're mine. Only mine.)

She came again, broken and wild and perfect.

I followed, a groan tearing from my throat, filling her, losing myself.

And I didn't let go.

Not for a second.

Because tonight? She was *mine*.

Every inch.

Every cry.

Every sinful, ruined, perfect breath.

Her body was still trembling when I pulled her against my chest, breath ragged, skin flushed and marked in all the ways that made my blood pound. My hand slid up her spine, fingers splayed over her back like I could imprint myself on her.

"You okay?" I asked, voice low, lips at her temple.

Lexi let out a soft laugh, muffled against my neck. "Are you kidding?"

I smiled against her hair. But I wasn't done.

Not even close.

"Get up," I murmured, brushing her damp hair back.

She blinked, slow and dazed. "What?"

"I need you in the shower."

Her eyes widened slightly. "Again?"

I stood, grabbing her hand, dragging her with me. "You can still walk. Barely."

She trailed behind me, half-naked and glowing like sin. Her hoodie was on the floor, long forgotten. Her legs were wobbly, thighs trembling, and there were red fingerprints blooming over her hips and ass from where I'd held her too tight. Good. I wanted her marked. *Mine.*

Steam was already rising by the time I twisted the knob. I stepped in first, then pulled her in after me.

She gasped as the water hit her skin. Hot. Full blast. Surrounding us in a haze like we were the only two people on earth.

Her body was slick, wet, shining under the spray. And fuck me—I couldn't stop looking at her.

I pressed her back against the tile, hands flat beside her head, trapping her.

"Not done with you," I growled.

Lexi looked up at me, pupils blown, chest rising and falling like she knew exactly what was coming.

"You're obsessed," she whispered.

I kissed her. Hard. "Damn right I am."

My hands slid down, gripped her thighs, lifted her in one swift motion. She wrapped her legs around my waist like it was instinct.

I didn't wait.

I slid inside her slow—*so slow*—just to feel her stretch and shake and gasp. She was so hot, so tight, and I was already half-wild from the way she'd moaned my name minutes ago.

"Look at me," I demanded.

She did. Eyes wide, lips parted, water dripping down her flushed cheeks.

"You think that little attitude of yours doesn't have consequences?" I muttered, thrusting deep.

Lexi whimpered, head hitting the tile.

I kissed her neck, her collarbone, everywhere I could reach. My hands held her so tightly, she'd be bruised come morning. And I didn't care. I wanted those marks. I wanted her sore. Wanted her remembering me every time she shifted in her seat tomorrow.

Her nails scraped over my back, down my arms, clawing like she couldn't get close enough.

"You like being punished?" I whispered, thrusting harder. "You like getting spanked like a bad girl?"

She nodded, crying out.

"You keep testing me, I'll make a habit of it."

"Yes—yes, please, James..."

I growled, slamming into her, rhythm deep and brutal, her

cries echoing against the tile, water pounding around us like applause.

I felt her tighten, tremble, fall apart again with a strangled moan.

And then I followed.

Teeth clenched, body shaking, spilling inside her with a growl so loud it didn't even sound human.

We stayed there, bodies tangled, steam curling around us like smoke from a fire neither of us wanted to put out.

When I finally pulled back, she was panting, completely wrecked, lips swollen, hair plastered to her face—and smiling.

That smug little grin that always undid me.

"You're insatiable," she whispered, voice hoarse.

I kissed her one more time, slow and deep.

"Only for you."

* * *

Her legs were still wrapped around my waist, arms around my neck like she wasn't ready to let go—and truthfully, neither was I.

She was warm and slick in my arms, her breath fluttering against my neck, her body heavy with exhaustion and the kind of satisfaction that turned my chest to ash.

I adjusted my grip on her thighs and pulled back just enough to see her face.

Eyes closed. Lips parted.

Ruined.

Beautiful.

Completely fucking mine.

"I've got you," I whispered, kissing her temple. "Let's get

you dry."

She murmured something against my skin—nonsense and vowels—but didn't let go.

I smiled, a rare thing, something soft just for her. Then I unwrapped her legs and set her down gently, holding her steady while she blinked through the haze. Her body trembled slightly under my hands, and I wrapped an arm around her waist, guiding her out of the shower like she was made of glass and gold.

I grabbed a towel and ran it over her skin, slow and methodical, catching every drop as if the water dared to linger on what belonged to me.

She stood quietly, letting me take care of her, letting me see her undone like this.

"Sit," I said gently, patting the edge of the bed.

Lexi did, robe slipping down one shoulder as she perched there, flushed and dazed.

I dropped to one knee in front of her, towel still in hand, and dried her feet, her calves, slow like worship.

"Why are you being sweet?" she asked, voice barely above a whisper. "Did I hit my head?"

I looked up at her, brow raised. "You think I wreck you and then just leave you like roadkill?"

She smiled, that sleepy, post-orgasm smirk that made something twist in my chest. "I mean, kinda."

"Brat," I muttered, standing to grab one of the thick hotel robes. I held it open. "Arms up."

She obeyed. Smugly. Slowly. On purpose.

I slid the robe over her shoulders, then rubbed her arms through the terry cloth like I was trying to warm her with friction alone.

Then I wrapped her up and lifted her into bed.

"Wow," she mumbled, curling into the sheets. "Do you also offer breakfast and emotional stability?"

"Just the first one," I said, tucking the blanket around her. "The emotional part's still in beta testing."

She laughed—quiet, breathy, the sound of someone completely at peace.

I disappeared into the bathroom for a minute, wiped myself down, threw on a pair of sweats, and grabbed two bottles of water from the minibar. When I came back, she was almost asleep.

I slid in beside her and placed the water on the nightstand. Then pulled her into my chest.

Lexi let out a soft, happy sigh and snuggled into me like she'd been doing it her whole life.

"You're warm," she mumbled.

"You're trouble."

Her fingers brushed over my chest, lazy and slow. "Same thing."

I kissed her hair. Just once. Just enough to let her know I wasn't letting go—not tonight.

She fell asleep like that. Curled against me. Breathing slow. Skin still carrying the ghost of everything we'd just done.

And I lay there in the dark, wide awake.

One arm wrapped around her.

One hand on the curve of her hip.

Heart a fucking mess.

Because even now, even after all of it—I still didn't know how I was going to let her go.

23

Chapter 23

Lexi

I left his room before sunrise.

No goodbye. No dramatic exit. Just the whisper of the door closing behind me and the echo of his hands still on my skin.

The hallway was empty. Silent, save for the distant hum of a vending machine and the soft padding of my hotel slippers on the carpet. My robe was cinched tight around me, and I had the walk-of-shame confidence of a woman who absolutely shouldn't be doing this—and might still do it again.

Of course I didn't make it halfway down the hall before I found Rachel.

Sitting cross-legged on the little loveseat by the elevator, sipping hotel coffee from a paper cup and scrolling her phone like this was normal. Like she hadn't absolutely planted herself there to catch me red-handed.

She didn't even look up.

"You're late," she said, flipping a page on her Kindle like she was some kind of suburban surveillance agent.

I groaned and slumped against the wall beside her. "What time is it?"

"Early. But not early enough to avoid me."

Of course it wasn't.

Rachel liked to come to away games. Said it was to support the team and "take advantage of her remote flexibility," but we both knew it was because she liked the drama—and the boys. She liked the buzz of a new city, the free drinks, and watching Connor stretch during warmups like it was a sport in itself. Rachel was chaos in a top knot, a one-woman hype team with no boundaries and an endless supply of ChapStick and hot takes.

I tried to slip past her. She stuck her leg out.

"Sit," she said.

I sat. Because I had no backbone, and she was stronger than she looked in yoga pants.

Rachel gave me a long, knowing look. That best-friend stare that cut through all my defenses like butter. "James?"

I hesitated. And that was answer enough.

She sipped her coffee like it was tea. "So. You've decided to sleep with the sexy Russian man who is, technically, your boss and definitely your ex's father. Bold strategy, Cotton."

I rubbed my face. "I didn't decide anything."

"Mmm." Sip. "So it just happened? Accidentally fell on his... leadership qualities?"

"Rachel."

She looked at me now. Really looked.

"Lex, I need to know—are you okay?"

I blinked.

"I mean it," she added. Sarcasm stripped away. "I know you want him. Hell, I can see it from orbit. But want isn't the same as ready. And this? This is messy. It could destroy everything if it gets out. You, him, Ethan—"

"I know."

Rachel fell quiet. Let the silence stretch.

"Is this gonna wreck you?"

My chest tightened.

Because I didn't know the answer to that.

Maybe.

Probably.

"Yes," I said quietly. "But I don't think I care anymore."

She reached over and squeezed my hand.

"Okay. Then we'll wreck together. I'll bring snacks."

I snorted. "Thanks."

"You know I've got a whole spreadsheet dedicated to the messes you make. Color-coded tabs and everything."

"Rachel—"

"Yours is pink. Mine is red. I put Maya in purple because she's an emotional wildcard."

I rolled my eyes. But the smile tugged at my lips anyway.

Rachel stood up and stretched, already snapping back into chaos mode. She cracked her neck like a seasoned veteran of emotionally compromised mornings.

"You've got thirty minutes to get your shit together. Game day, baby. Time to pretend you're a composed professional and not someone who was definitely just spanked by the head coach."

"Rachel—"

"Tell me I'm wrong."

I opened my mouth. Closed it.

She smirked. "Thought so."

And just like that, she tossed her coffee cup into the trash and strutted toward her room like she hadn't just lit my dignity on fire and roasted marshmallows over the flames.

God, I loved her.

* * *

The arena was loud. Packed. Charged with that first-road-game kind of energy that felt like it vibrated through your bones.

I moved through the chaos like I always did—headset on, camera crew prepped, notes in hand—but every step felt off. Like my balance had shifted and no one else noticed.

Because every time I looked up, he was there.

James.

Watching. Tracking my every move like he was still touching me. Like his fingerprints were still burned into my skin.

He said nothing. Did nothing.

But those eyes?

God, those eyes said everything.

Possession. Hunger. Restraint coiled so tight it looked like rage.

My face stayed neutral. My posture, professional. But under it all, my skin still buzzed from the way he'd held me just hours ago. From the way he'd made me forget who I was supposed to be.

The game itself was brutal.

Fast. Aggressive. The other team came in swinging, but our boys were locked in. Liam snagged an early goal, Ryan chirped his way through three penalties, and Connor was an actual wall in net. By the third period, the win was locked in—and the team was flying high.

James didn't smile. Not really. But I caught the way his jaw shifted, the twitch of his mouth. It was there. Barely. Like even he couldn't quite hold the wall.

And every time I passed him? That stare dug into me. Not soft. Not sweet. It pinned me in place and dared me to pretend last night didn't happen.

Afterward, the locker room was a zoo. I stood back with Rachel, laughing as the guys shouted over each other and dumped water on Ryan for "best on," even though Liam had scored twice and Connor had a shutout.

"Absolute bias," Liam said, mock-offended. "This team has no integrity."

"Yeah," Ryan shot back. "And your skating looks like Bambi on ice."

The room exploded with laughter.

Even Ethan cracked a grin, pulling his hoodie over his head as he tossed a towel at Ryan's face. "Tell that to the scoreboard, bro."

Rachel elbowed me. "Your ex is smiling. Is the world ending?"

I smiled. "Let's not jinx it."

Connor passed us shirtless on his way to the showers— muscles, tattoos, towel slung low—and Rachel's eyes followed him like she was about to write a thesis.

"He's art," she whispered.

"Have some shame," I whispered back.

"None left," she said. "Maybe I should make sure he's okay in the shower?"

I choked on my water.

Rachel grinned like she lived to break me.

The guys kept chirping, the noise and heat wrapping around

129

the space like victory itself. And for one second—just one—I forgot about everything else.

About the lines we were crossing. About the fallout. About the ache I was carrying for a man who never should've touched me.

Because right now, surrounded by these idiots, the people I actually chose—it felt like maybe everything would be okay.

24

Chapter 24

Lexi

The hum of the plane was steady. Calm. The kind of quiet that settled in after a win, after the adrenaline faded and the players were too tired to chirp or wrestle over armrests. Most of the team was half-asleep. A few were watching movies, a few scrolling their phones. Rachel had her hood up and was pretending not to drool on her neck pillow.

I'd just closed my eyes when I felt it.

A presence.

I looked up—and there he was.

Ethan.

Standing in the aisle beside me, hands shoved in his hoodie pocket, expression unreadable.

"Can I sit?"

I blinked. "Uh. Sure."

He dropped into the empty seat beside me, silent for a beat. The kind of silent that weighed *heavy*.

"I've been trying to figure out how to do this," he said finally.

My heart thudded once. Loud. Obnoxious.

"Then don't," I said softly, already bracing for impact. "It's fine, Ethan. We don't have to—"

"No," he cut in, voice low. "We do. I need to say it."

People were listening. Not *obviously*. But I caught the way Liam went still a few rows back. The way Ryan casually took out one AirPod and didn't put it back in. Even Rachel cracked one eye open under her hoodie.

And James?

I didn't have to look to know he was watching. I *felt* it. Like a static charge from the front of the plane.

Ethan cleared his throat, leaned forward slightly, elbows on his knees. "I was an idiot. You know that. I know that. Everyone *knows* that."

He kept going.

"I messed up. Worse than I ever thought I could. I hurt you, and I didn't even have the guts to face it after. Just... ran. Avoided it. Like a coward. I know we kind of spoke at the club but I just needed to make sure we cleared the air."

He wasn't looking at me. His gaze was on the floor between his feet.

I swallowed, my voice thin. "Why now?"

"Because I miss you," he said, finally looking at me. "Not like that. I'm not trying to win you back. I just... I miss being able to make you laugh. Miss talking to you. And this season's going so well. The energy's good. The guys are solid. And we work *together*, Lex. We can't keep pretending it's not weird."

I smiled. Small. Sad. "You were kind of an asshole."

He laughed, breathless. "Yeah. I was."

We sat in that silence for a second—raw, honest, weirdly calm.

"So," he said. "Can we... start over? Not like a clean slate, I don't expect that. But friends? Or... co-workers who don't actively want to poison each other's coffee?"

I gave him a long look.

Ethan. My first real heartbreak. My biggest disappointment. The guy who wrecked me—and now looked like he'd finally grown up just enough to regret it.

And still... it felt done. Not unfinished. Not unresolved.

Just... done.

I nodded. "Friends."

Relief flooded his face. "Thank god."

Then—because this is Ethan—we fist bumped. Like we were twelve.

He stood and stretched. "Alright. That was the hardest thing I've done in a year. I'm gonna go sit with Coach before I lose all my nerve."

My breath caught.

James.

Ethan must've seen the flicker in my expression, because he hesitated. "Yeah... I know. That's weird too. But I meant it when I said I'm trying. He's trying too. We're figuring it out. I think me and my dad might have a chance to rebuild something."

I nodded once, not trusting myself to speak.

Ethan gave me a look—half smile, half something softer. Then he turned and walked up the aisle.

Right to the front.

Right to James.

And sat down beside him.

Neither of them said anything at first. But I watched James shift slightly in his seat, angling toward Ethan. Not cold. Not hostile.

Just... open. Guarded, but open.

My heart twisted.

Because I didn't know what scared me more—losing them both...

Or getting caught in the middle again.

25

Chapter 25

James

I saw them before they saw me.

Lexi. Ethan.

He slid into the seat beside her with this easy, familiar comfort—like he hadn't spent months avoiding her, like he hadn't been chewing on guilt since the start of the season. And she turned toward him with that smile—the soft one, the one that hit like a punch to the chest.

It lit something dark in me. Possessive. Ugly. Primal.

I gritted my teeth and stared out the window like it held the cure for whatever sickness she was working into my bloodstream. I was doing better. I was keeping distance. I was making good decisions.

And then he stood.

And walked toward me.

For a second, I thought he'd changed his mind. That whatever progress he'd made with Lexi had pushed him further away from me.

But then he stopped right at my row.

"Mind if I sit?" he asked.

I blinked. "Sure."

He dropped into the seat beside me, gangly and casual like we weren't about to have a conversation that could shatter both of us. He didn't fidget. Didn't flinch. Just sat, hands resting loosely on his thighs, eyes forward.

Silence stretched.

Then, without looking at me, he said, "I know you sent money."

My shoulders stiffened.

"But why weren't you ever around?"

I exhaled slowly. Stared at the back of the seat in front of me. A thousand memories flooded my mind—airport gates I never went through, phone calls that ended before they rang, birthday presents returned unopened.

I weighed every possible answer.

"I tried," I said eventually. "Believe it or not, I tried. But your mom... she made it hard."

He didn't speak. Just waited.

"I'm not going to badmouth her," I added. "But she didn't want me around. Told me you'd be better off without me. And... I believed her."

His jaw flexed. Just once.

"I didn't stay away because I didn't care, Ethan. I stayed away because every time I tried to fight for you, it got worse. Lawyers. Press threats. Public image bullshit. I thought I was protecting you."

I paused, remembering the first time I saw his picture in a magazine—seven years old, all dimples and defiance. My son. And I was watching him grow up from hotel rooms and private tabs. I'd bought every jersey he ever wore. Watched every game he ever played. Always from the shadows.

"You should've fought harder," he said. Quiet. Firm. But not cruel.

"I know."

And I did. That was the worst part. I knew I failed him.

He let that hang. Then nodded once. "Thank you for saying it."

I wasn't sure what hurt more—his forgiveness or the fact that I didn't feel like I deserved it.

We sat in silence again, the hum of the plane settling around us. Most of the team was dozing or plugged into headphones. Lexi hadn't looked back. But I could feel her presence like gravity. Like guilt.

"She's coming back next week," Ethan said suddenly.

I turned. "Who?"

"My mom."

Sabine.

"Wants to come to a few games. Be involved. Show support or whatever."

I said nothing. Just clenched my jaw hard enough to ache.

"And..." he added, a little cautious now, "she asked if we'd all get dinner. Like, the three of us."

My entire body tensed.

Dinner with Sabine. The woman who tore me from him, leveraged our son as a bargaining chip, and played the press like a puppet string. She didn't want reconciliation—she wanted headlines.

"She wants something," I muttered.

"She always wants something," Ethan said. "But I'd like you to come. I think it's time."

Time for what? For a carefully orchestrated PR reunion? A chance for Sabine to get her face in the press again and remind everyone who she used to be?

But Ethan looked at me—not with naivety. Not with expectation. Just... with hope. And that was worse. Because I knew what hope did. I knew what happened when it shattered.

And still—I nodded slowly. "I'll be there."

"Thanks," he said. Then added, "It's not just for her. I want this to work, too."

He stood a moment later, stretching his legs before moving toward the front of the cabin. But before he left, he hesitated— just a beat—and added, almost under his breath, "I'm working on it. On me. I know I've screwed things up. I know I've hurt people. But I'm trying. I don't want to be the guy who keeps letting people down and I would really like to explore our relationship some more."

His voice cracked a little on that last part, and something inside me twisted.

Because I believed him.

For the first time, I really, truly believed that Ethan wasn't just saying what he thought I wanted to hear. He was trying to make amends. Not just with me. With himself. He passed Lexi on the way. Didn't touch her. Didn't even pause.

But I saw her glance up.

And in that moment, something shifted.

Something big.

Something dangerous.

Because I was finally starting to get my son back.

And I didn't know how the hell I was going to keep him— without losing her.

And for the first time since she walked into my life, I didn't know if I could survive the cost of choosing one over the other.

26

Chapter 26

Lexi

It had been exactly a few days since I last saw James.

And even though I'd spent the week *trying* to be good—burying myself in prep meetings, scouting footage, player interviews, and pretending I wasn't unravelling every time I saw his name on the group schedule—none of it helped. Not really.

I was holding it together by sheer force of will. Barely.

It helped that he'd been doing the same—professional to the point of being cold. Not a glance, not a slip. If I hadn't had the memory of his mouth between my thighs like a ghost, I could've convinced myself it never happened.

But it did.

And now it was game day again. A home game. The first one since... well, everything.

The arena buzzed with energy, media teams flying around, fans flooding in, players chirping each other in the tunnel. I moved through the chaos like usual—headphones in, clipboard under my arm, focused. Steady.

Until I saw her.

Sabine.

Ethan's mother.

Glamorous. Tall. Blonde. Draped in some oversized designer coat that probably cost more than my car. She had sunglasses on indoors, lipstick too perfect, and a smile that didn't quite reach her eyes.

And she was walking in beside Ethan like they were the goddamn royal family.

My stomach dropped.

I hadn't expected her to show up this early—if anything, I thought she'd breeze in mid-season with fanfare and a camera crew. But no, here she was. Effortlessly perfect. And clearly here to play a role.

They walked straight toward the media gate, laughing at something I couldn't hear. Ethan looked... calm. Maybe even happy. And for that, I was glad. I was. Really.

Right up until he spotted me.

"Lexi!" he called, waving me over casually.

Sabine turned as I approached, her eyes narrowing just slightly.

"Hey," I said, smile glued on, trying not to look like I wanted to evaporate.

"This is my mom," Ethan said. "Sabine."

"Lexi," she repeated, extending a hand. Her voice was honeyed and smooth—charming, practiced. "I've heard so much about you."

I shook her hand, which was soft and warm and had just enough grip to feel like a warning.

"Likewise," I lied.

And then James appeared.

Of course.

He came in from the player tunnel, clipboard in hand, earpiece in, looking all business—until he saw the three of us. His eyes caught mine first, just for a breath. Then they landed on Sabine.

And the mask he wore was instant.

"Sabine," he said, voice a notch too polite.

She lit up like a power surge. "James. *Darling.*"

And then she kissed his cheek. Both cheeks.

I stood there, frozen in time, trying not to visibly choke on my own shock.

She touched his arm like they were old friends. Lovers. Royalty reunited. And James... he just took it. Barely flinching. Emotionless.

"Still as handsome as ever," she purred.

I wanted to scream.

Instead, I smiled tightly and stepped back. "I should get back to pre-game. Excuse me."

James didn't stop me. Ethan didn't notice.

But Sabine?

Sabine watched me go like she already knew everything.

And god, I hated how much I wanted to turn around and slap that perfectly glossy smirk right off her face.

I escaped the lobby like it was on fire.

Which, emotionally speaking, it was.

Sabine's perfume still clung to the hallway like expensive sabotage. Her voice, her hand on James's arm, the way she laughed like she hadn't casually wrecked an entire family and then strutted back into the building like it was her personal stage.

God. I needed air.

Instead, I got the players' tunnel, the bench cameras, a buzzing headset, and an arena full of screaming fans.

Focus. I just needed to focus.

The home opener had that kind of energy that got in your bones—adrenaline and nostalgia wrapped in organ music and the smell of popcorn. I checked on the camera crews, nodded to the broadcasters, made sure the pre-game light show was queued perfectly.

Busy. Sharp. Unbothered.

I even managed to avoid James entirely for the rest of warm-up, which was both a win and a tragedy.

By the time the puck dropped, I was fully in professional mode. Eyes on the team. Mic keyed in. Heart safely locked behind a steel vault of denial.

And yet...

I still felt him.

I always felt him.

From across the bench. From the coaching zone. From wherever he stood with his arms crossed, calling line changes like he wasn't also silently dragging his eyes across my body every chance he got.

I didn't look at him. Much.

Okay, maybe a little.

And if he happened to catch my gaze across the glass and hold it just long enough to make me forget how to breathe?

Well. That was my problem.

We won. Obviously.

The crowd was deafening. The boys were cocky and golden

and exactly the brand of chaos we needed.

Rachel was at the glass during the final buzzer, hammering it like a possessed fangirl, screaming Connor's name like she hadn't been pretending she *wasn't into him* for three months straight.

Liam skated past and blew her a kiss. Ryan tossed his stick over the glass. Even Ethan was grinning ear to ear, tapping his helmet in my direction like we were friends again.

And me?

I was smiling. Genuinely. Because despite everything—the jealousy, the sabotage, the wildly inappropriate tension—I loved this team.

Even when they were emotionally exhausting and chronically shirtless.

"Post-game drinks at our place?" Rachel asked, bumping into my side as I packed up the equipment list.

"I should say no," I muttered, scribbling something on the clipboard.

"But you won't," she sang.

She was right. I wouldn't.

Because I had too much energy to burn and too many feelings I wasn't allowed to feel.

And no amount of pretending could keep the burn at bay forever.

* * *

I wasn't following them. Let's make that clear.

I was walking out of the arena. Like a normal person. A tired, emotionally drained, entirely dignified media coordinator who absolutely wasn't spiralling over her boss and his terrifyingly beautiful *maybe-still-somehow-wife.*

And then I saw them.

At the far end of the lobby. James, Sabine, and Ethan.

Together.

Laughing.

Ethan had his hand on her back, steering her toward the doors. She was glowing in some tailored designer thing with a bag that probably cost more than my rent, and James was... smiling.

That hurt the most.

Not the fake polite press smile. The *real* one. The one that was rare and a little crooked and almost impossible to look away from.

I froze.

Of course I did.

Because how do you casually walk past the man who ruined you with his mouth and then ignored you for a week—while he's heading out for family dinner with his ex and son like you didn't exist?

Answer: You don't. You stand there like a deer in the headlights of your own pathetic decisions.

And then—because of course—Ethan noticed me.

"Lexi!" he called out, smiling as if this wasn't the world's worst timing. "Hey, you remember my mom, right?"

I remembered her *ankle-breaking* heels and blood-red lip-stick.

Sabine turned toward me with a smile that didn't reach her eyes. "Of course. Lovely to see you again."

I blinked. "You too."

James hadn't said a word. He just stood there, tall and unreadable, his hands shoved in the pockets of his coat like he couldn't trust them.

I didn't look at him.

Much.

Just enough to catch the subtle twitch in his jaw and the way his eyes tracked every inch of me.

I straightened my shoulders. "Have a nice dinner."

And then I walked away—heels clicking, spine straight, smile frozen.

I didn't cry. Not in the elevator. Not in the hallway. Not until the door to my apartment closed behind me.

27

Chapter 27

James

I knew I'd made a mistake the second we stepped out of the car.

Not because the restaurant screamed *old money and deeper secrets*, though it did. And not because Sabine made a scene with the valet like she was arriving for a red carpet premiere. No—the mistake was saying yes at all.

The drive over had been civil. Barely.

Ethan talked just enough to keep things from slipping into full silence. Sabine sat in the back beside me, legs crossed, scrolling through her phone like she couldn't be bothered unless the paparazzi were already waiting.

And me? I spent the entire ride thinking about Lexi.

Thinking about how she looked tonight on the sidelines— confident, sharp, impossible to look away from. Thinking about the way she smiled at Ethan when he scored, like it still meant something. Thinking about how every second I spent in Sabine's orbit made me want to run the hell back into hers.

But I didn't.

Because I was here for Ethan.

We reached the restaurant, and Sabine hooked her arm through mine like this was some staged reconciliation dinner for *Hello! Magazine.* The maître d' greeted her like an old friend—which told me all I needed to know about the type of places she still frequented.

"James," she said sweetly, turning to face me as we were led to the table. "Try not to look so grim. We're celebrating."

"Celebrating what?" I asked. "Our collective ability to pretend?"

Her smile didn't falter. "You always were such a killjoy."

I bit my tongue.

We sat. She beside me. Ethan across.

The table was a mirror—three reflections of a broken history. Sabine sparkled. Ethan glowed with cautious hope. And I— well, I was just trying not to crack under the weight of old mistakes and new regrets.

Ethan passed me a menu with a hopeful grin. "Thought it'd be good for us to do this. You know... like a family."

I gave him a nod. "I'm here."

Sabine reached for her wine glass with a manicured hand that sparkled with rings I probably still paid for. "It's been too long," she said. "Do you remember that little place in Prague we used to go to after your away games?"

"I remember the games," I said.

Her smile twitched.

Ethan jumped in, eager to bridge the awkward gap. "Mom still talks about those trips like they were the best years of her life."

Of course she did. Revisionist history was her superpower.

The wine kept flowing. The food arrived. Sabine dominated the conversation with carefully selected nostalgia and high-effort charm. She laughed at my jokes like it meant something. Dropped compliments like flower petals. Brushed her fingers across my wrist like it was an accident.

It wasn't.

She was toying with the idea of us. Or at least the image of it. She always did love a well-lit illusion.

And Ethan—he kept trying. Asking questions. Steering us back to "what ifs" and "do you ever wonders." He wanted something he could salvage. A family photo to mentally reframe and hang on a wall that didn't exist.

I gave polite answers. Neutral. Careful.

Because I wasn't here to rehash. I wasn't here to blame.

I was here for Ethan.

But my mind was somewhere else. Someone else.

And when the waiter walked away with our dessert order, Sabine leaned in, just enough for her perfume to sting.

"We were good together once, weren't we?"

I stared at her hand, resting lightly on my sleeve.

"We were a lot of things," I said. "But we weren't right."

Her lips curled like she knew better. "Maybe we could be again. For Ethan."

That was her angle. Of course it was.

Before I could respond, I pulled out my phone and opened a text thread that grounded me like nothing else could.

James:

Made it through the appetizer. Barely. How's your evening?

It took a minute before the reply buzzed through.
Lexi:
Oh, you know. Just curled up with a book. Hope your family dinner is everything you dreamed.
That one hit harder than I expected.
James:
It's not. I keep thinking about you.
Lexi:
Don't. Not tonight.

I stared at the screen.

And didn't push back.

"Who's that?" Ethan asked casually, glancing at my phone.

"Just a friend."

He nodded, too quickly. He clocked it.

Dinner dragged. Sabine got looser with the wine, bolder with the comments. The flirtation ramped up in subtle, uncomfortable ways. And I stayed frozen in place, expression carved from stone.

Until finally, finally, the bill came.

We stepped out into the cool night, the restaurant's golden glow behind us, the air sharp with late autumn chill. Ethan pulled out his phone.

"I've got a car coming."

"Thanks for tonight," he added, glancing between us. "It meant a lot."

I clapped a hand on his shoulder. "Anything for you, son."

He smiled—genuine, small, but there—and turned toward the cab as it rolled to the curb.

Sabine waited until the door shut.

Then turned to me.

"Walk me to my car?"

I should've said no. But I didn't.

We walked in silence, her heels clicking against the pavement like punctuation marks.

She stopped beside the driver's side, leaned back, arms crossed lightly. "Tonight felt good, didn't it?"

"No," I said. "It felt necessary."

She gave me a pitying smile. "You always were so dramatic."

"Sabine."

She stepped closer. "Why don't we go back to your hotel? For old times' sake."

I looked at her.

Not angry. Just done.

"I'll do anything for Ethan," I said. "But don't mistake that for hope. Whatever we were—it's done. And it never should've lasted as long as it did."

Her expression hardened, even if her lips stayed smiling. "You really mean that."

"I should've said it years ago."

She stepped back, finally, hand slipping into her coat. "At least you're honest."

"I always was," I said. "You just never liked the answers."

She climbed into her car without another word.

I stood on the curb, watching her pull away into the night.

And for the first time in a long time, I didn't feel conflicted.

I just felt ready.

I pulled out my phone. Thumb hovering over Lexi's name.

But I didn't text her again.

Not yet.

Not while I still had blood from another battle on my hands.

Because the next move I made?

It couldn't be another mistake.
It had to be her.
And it had to be right.

28

Chapter 28

Lexi

I was curled up on the couch with a half-empty mug of wine and a full-blown existential crisis.

He was with her.

Playing happy families.

Rachel had abandoned her laptop in favor of watching me unravel.

"He's not your boyfriend," she said gently, legs tucked under her as she scrolled aimlessly through her phone.

"I know that."

"You told him to have a nice time with his family."

"I know that too."

"And yet..." she gestured vaguely toward me, "here you are. Pouting like a Disney princess whose prince went to the ball with his ex-wife."

"She was never his wife."

"Oh, I'm sorry, does that make it better?"

I didn't answer. Because it didn't. Not really.

I didn't know what was worse—the fact that I was jealous, or the fact that I had no idea what I was even jealous of. Sabine had the history. The kid. The memories. I had... what? A few months' worth of dirty secrets?

That wasn't love. I don't think.

It wasn't even smart.

But it was something. And that something felt like it was unraveling by the minute.

I tugged James's hoodie tighter around me and stared out the window.

He was probably still at dinner, drinking overpriced wine and smiling politely at the woman who once made it her life's mission to ruin him.

I took a sip of wine. Made a face. It was warm. Of course it was.

That's when my phone lit up.

James Volkov.

I stared at the name for a second, like it might bite. Then I answered, because apparently I have no self-preservation.

"Hello?"

A pause. Then—

"Tell me you're not wearing my hoodie while thinking about how badly you want to hurt me."

My heart stuttered. His voice was low. Rough. The kind of voice that left bruises.

"Hmm. You should be at dinner," I muttered.

"I was," he said. "Didn't feel like pretending any longer."

"Why?"

Silence. Heavy. Tense. Then—

"Because I couldn't stop wondering if you were thinking about me while I was trying to forget you."

I closed my eyes. The weight of his voice pressed into my skin like a hand on my throat.

"Don't say that."

"Why not?"

"Because you're not supposed to call me at midnight and tell me that while you're playing happy family with your ex and your son."

"She's not my ex," he snapped, voice suddenly edged.

I flinched. He caught it.

"I know you're pissed."

"I'm not pissed," I lied. "I'm fine."

I looked over at Rachel, who was eavesdropping like it was her full-time job. I threw a pillow at her. She caught it. Didn't even blink.

"I wanted to call you the second we sat down," he said. "But I didn't want to lose what little control I had left."

"You've never called me before."

"Because talking to you like this makes it harder to pretend I can stay away."

I sucked in a breath.

"I miss you."

"I miss you too," I whispered.

"Can I see you tomorrow?"

"Are you asking or telling?"

His voice darkened. Dropped to a rasp. "I'm trying to ask. But I'm not going to beg. You know what I want. You've always known."

My pulse throbbed.

"Tomorrow."

"Good."

Another beat. Then—

"I don't do soft, Lexi. I don't do light. But I would burn down the world for you."

"You should scare me."

"You should be scared of what I'd do to protect you. But not of me. Never of me."

My throat tightened.

"Goodnight, Lexi."

"Goodnight, Volkov."

He hung up.

I stared at the screen, my hands trembling, every inch of me lit with something electric and wrong and right all at once.

Rachel threw the pillow back at me.

"He's terrifying."

"Yeah."

"But like...hot terrifying."

I groaned.

"You're not done, are you?"

"Not even close."

She smirked. "Knew it. I'll prep the emotional damage snacks."

I leaned my head against the couch and closed my eyes.

Tomorrow was going to be war.

And I was walking into it willingly.

29

Chapter 29

Lexi

The text came in just after seven.

> **James:** *No game this week. Come away with me for a couple of days.*

Just like that. No context. No emoji. Not even a question mark. Just a command, disguised as a request.

I blinked at it, still wrapped in my duvet, brain only half awake.

Then it buzzed again.

> **James:** *I know it's a terrible idea. I just think maybe we need a reset. Get this out of our systems. Or figure out if it's more than that.*

My heart did a full gymnastics routine.

It should've been a no. It should've been an absolutely not, you complicated, gorgeous, emotionally dangerous man. But instead...

> **Me:** *Where are we going?*
> **James:** *I'll pick you up in an hour. Be ready.*

James pulled up like a storm in human form.

Black jeans, dark sweater, sunglasses like he was daring the sky to challenge him. Effortless. Dangerous. Designed to unravel me.

I slid into the passenger seat, my bag hitting the floor with a thud. I tried to act like it didn't contain an irresponsible amount of lingerie and one dress that screamed: I know better but I don't care.

He didn't look at me right away. Just reached over and handed me coffee—my exact order, made like it was muscle memory.

Then he turned.

His eyes dragged over me—hoodie, leggings, sleep-creased ponytail—and stopped at my mouth.

"You're late," I said, because if I didn't say something, I might melt.

"You're lucky I didn't change my mind."

"Would've been safer."

"You didn't sign up for safe," he said. Then added, quieter, "You signed up for me."

I buckled my seatbelt. "We doing this or not?"

He smirked, eyes on the road. "Try and stop me."

The engine roared to life.

And just like that, we were off.

We left the city fast—highways blurring into forest roads, trees swaying in the wind like they knew we shouldn't be doing this either.

"So," I said after a while. "Where exactly are we going?"

"My cabin."

Of course he had a cabin.

"Remote. Private. No reporters. No distractions."

"No witnesses," I muttered.

James smirked. "Wouldn't that be convenient."

He didn't say anything for a while after that, and I let the silence stretch, letting the scenery wash over me. It was beautiful—too beautiful. Like the universe was trying to distract us with pretty things while we made bad choices.

By the time we pulled up the long gravel drive, I'd nearly talked myself out of the entire thing.

And then I saw the cabin.

Correction: **The Cabin.**

It looked like a cinematic backdrop for a forbidden romance novel. Dark wood. Stone chimney. Giant windows. A porch that wrapped around like it had something to prove.

"You have got to be kidding me," I whispered.

James killed the engine and looked over at me. "What?"

"This is not a cabin. This is a luxury escape for people who do crimes and then go off the grid."

He shrugged. "There's coffee inside."

I stepped out into the crisp mountain air, my boots crunching against the gravel. "If you try to seduce me with a Chemex and wood-burning fireplace, I will sue you."

"No lies up here," he said, grabbing our bags. "You knew what this was."

I did.

And it still didn't prepare me for the hot tub. Or the fireplace. Or the interior that looked like it had been ripped out of Architectural Digest and set to the playlist titled '*Oops, We Fell in Love in the Mountains.*'

I walked through the living room with wide eyes, every corner more aggressively cozy than the last.

"This place is a trap."

James dropped our bags by the stairs. "I'm a man of simple tastes."

"Simple?" I said, turning in a slow circle. "This couch cost more than my rent."

He tossed me a throw blanket. "Then sit on it. Get your money's worth."

By the time we were curled up with wine on the couch—blankets and banter between us—I was already spiraling. Not in the bad way. In the *I forgot how easy it is to be around you and I hate it* way.

"Tell me something I don't know," I said.

James raised a brow. "About what?"

"You. A deep, dark secret. Or like… a weird hobby," I said, raising an eyebrow over my wine glass.

James didn't flinch. "I race cars."

I blinked. "Like… on the freeway when someone cuts you off?"

"No," he said dryly. "On tracks. With rules. And helmets."

I nearly choked. "You're telling me you voluntarily drive 200 miles an hour for fun?"

"I'm telling you it's the only time my brain shuts up, other than when I'm on the ice."

I stared at him. "Okay, that's actually insane."

He smirked, slow and unapologetic. "You asked for a weird

160

hobby."

"That's not a hobby," I said. "That's a cry for help with a high insurance premium."

James leaned in, eyes dark. "You ever been in a car going that fast?"

"No."

"Then don't knock it," he said, voice low and dangerous. "There's something about giving up control. Letting the speed take over. It's addictive. One day I'll take you."

I was definitely spiralling now.

He leaned in, voice low. "Want to know what else is unexpected?"

I blinked. "What?"

"How badly I've wanted to do this."

He kissed me then—slow and devastating and unfair. My heart thundered, every thought in my head replaced with the feeling of his mouth on mine.

When we broke apart, I was breathless.

"This is a terrible idea," I whispered.

"Definitely," he said, already pulling me into his lap. "We should do it again."

I curled into him, letting the moment swallow me whole.

There were no rules up here.

No timelines. No roles.

Just us.

And that... that was the most dangerous part of all.

Because down in the real world, I could pretend this wasn't real. I could compartmentalize—convince myself it was all just heat and timing and long stretches of eye contact we weren't supposed to make. But up here? With the fire crackling and his arms around me and his heartbeat steady against my cheek?

James's fingers skimmed my thigh, slow and unhurried. Lazy, like he had hours to burn and no intention of doing anything except getting lost in me.

"I like you like this," he said quietly.

I tilted my head to look up at him. "Like what?"

He traced a line from my knee to the hem of my oversized hoodie. His hoodie. "Soft. Unfiltered. Not trying so hard to pretend you're unaffected."

I swallowed hard. "That goes both ways."

He smiled, barely there. But his eyes?

Dark.

Dangerous.

Hungry.

"You really want to know what I'm pretending?" he asked, voice low, breath brushing the shell of my ear.

I nodded, pulse jumping.

"I'm pretending I can let you go after this."

My breath caught.

"I'm pretending," he continued, "that this is a break. That we're resetting. That I'll be able to walk away when we get back."

My heart was thudding so hard I was sure he could feel it. "And you can't?"

He shook his head, slow and deliberate. "Not even a little."

* * *

The fire crackled softly, casting a golden glow across the living room. The wine was half gone. So was my resolve.

I'd curled into one corner of the couch, legs tucked beneath me, half-listening as James told a story about a ridiculous preseason trip in Russia that ended with a brawl, two goats, and a very stern warning from the KHL commissioner.

He was laughing now—*actually laughing*—and it hit me in a way I wasn't expecting.

He didn't laugh like that around other people.

Maybe not at all.

And the way he looked at me when he did?

Like I was the only person in the world who'd ever made him feel *light.*

I shifted, leaning back into the cushions, letting the moment stretch. "So let me get this straight—you, a six-foot-two professional athlete, were chased by a goat?"

"It was an *aggressive* goat," he said, trying not to smile. "It had very personal issues."

"Oh yeah?" I grinned. "And did it headbutt your pride or just your shins?"

He gave me a look. "It headbutted my knee and I'm pretty sure it still haunts me."

I was laughing, full and unfiltered, when he suddenly leaned closer—just enough to shift the air between us.

Not touching.

Not yet.

But the spark was instant.

I was still catching my breath from laughing when the shift happened—his eyes darker now, his voice quieter, the space between us charged.

"I like when you laugh," he said, his gaze locked on mine.

The compliment settled warm and heavy in my chest, but I forced myself to sit back slightly, pretending to play it cool. "So," I said, trying to deflect, "what do you actually *do* now?

You know, besides temporarily coach hockey teams and lure unsuspecting women into suspiciously romantic mountain cabins?"

His mouth curved into a slow, dangerous smile. "Suspiciously romantic, huh?"

"I've seen two throw blankets and a fireplace. This is a rom-com setup, Volkov. Don't play dumb."

He shook his head, amused. "I should've known you'd call me out."

"Obviously. Now answer the question."

He leaned back, stretching his arm across the back of the couch—his hand landing just behind my shoulders. Casual. Infuriating.

"Right before I retired," he said, "I invested in a nightclub chain with a few guys I knew from the league. At the time, I thought it'd be a one-off."

"Wait, you own *nightclubs?*"

He nodded. "Now I've got eleven of them. Across the U.S. and Canada. All upscale. Private. Very... low-profile."

I blinked. "That's... unexpected."

"Why?"

"I don't know," I said, tilting my head. "You don't seem like the 'bottle service and VIP booth' type."

He smirked. "I'm not. But I *am* the 'make sure the lighting's flattering and the liquor's premium' type. It's business."

I studied him for a beat, a thousand questions spinning through my brain. He'd never brought it up before. Not once. Not during the games, not during press calls, not even after we'd... well. You know.

"So let me get this straight," I said, narrowing my eyes. "You're a retired hockey star turned nightclub mogul... and you *still* make time to be aggressively broody and emotionally unavailable?"

James chuckled, low and warm. "I'm a man of many talents."

I rolled my eyes. "You're a walking contradiction."

"Funny," he said, his voice dropping an octave. "That's exactly how I'd describe you."

I swallowed hard. Because the way he was looking at me now? Like he wasn't just seeing me—he was *reading* me. Undressing me with nothing but his eyes and a devastating amount of restraint.

My heart thundered in my chest.

"You keep looking at me like that," I said, voice barely above a whisper, "and I'm not going to be responsible for what happens next."

His hand brushed lightly against my shoulder. "What if I *want* to see what happens next?"

His fingers traced a slow, barely-there line along the back of my shoulder.

I should've moved.

I should've backed away.

Instead, I turned toward him—just enough to meet his gaze head-on.

His hand moved—slow, deliberate—curling around the side of my neck, thumb brushing just beneath my jaw. My breath caught, and I hated how much I loved that he could do that to me with barely a touch.

He leaned in until our foreheads touched, his breath warm on my lips. "You drive me crazy, kotyonok."

"Stop calling me that," I murmured.

"Why?"

"Because every time you say it..." I swallowed hard. "I forget all the reasons I shouldn't want you."

His lips brushed mine—soft, tentative, like he was still giving me an out.

I didn't take it.

Instead, I surged forward and kissed him like I meant it.

And he kissed me back like he'd been waiting days to do it.

His hand slid into my hair, tilting my head as he deepened the kiss, hungry and possessive. I gasped into his mouth, clutching the front of his shirt, already half on fire and nowhere near ready to stop.

We moved without thinking—my back hitting the couch cushions, his body coming over mine, strong and solid and *too much* in the best way.

"I tried to stay away from you," he murmured against my neck, his lips brushing the skin just beneath my ear. "I really fucking tried."

"I didn't want you to," I whispered.

His mouth crashed back onto mine, and the last bit of space between us disappeared completely.

Hands roamed. Clothes shifted. Breathless gasps filled the air as we gave in, again, to the one thing we couldn't seem to quit.

He wasn't careful this time.

He wasn't slow.

He kissed me like a man who had finally stopped pretending.

And I held onto him like I was never letting go.

He didn't waste time.

One second, I was pinned to the couch, his mouth devouring mine like he was starving—and the next, he was pulling me to my feet, spinning me around, pressing my back flat against the cabin wall.

He pinned me to the cabin wall with enough force to rattle the frame. One hand gripped my hip, dragging me into him like he was trying to fuse us together. The other slid up, wrapping lightly around my throat—enough to claim, to command, to make my knees weaken without him even applying pressure.

His mouth found mine, all hunger and fury and intent.

I gasped, and he took that too—swallowing the sound like it belonged to him.

"Hands up," he growled against my lips.

I obeyed instantly, breath catching as I flattened my palms against the cold wood behind me.

"Good girl," he muttered, voice like velvet soaked in gasoline. "Now don't move."

He stepped in closer—chest to chest, thigh between my legs—his eyes black with something feral. Something possessive. Something just this side of dangerous.

His hand tightened slightly on my throat, not choking, just reminding me who I belonged to.

"You like this," he said. Not a question. A fact. "You like being at my mercy. You like knowing I could break you in half and you'd still beg me not to stop."

I whimpered.

He kissed me again, rougher this time—teeth scraping, lips bruising. His free hand roamed down, slipping beneath the hem of my hoodie, fingers dragging heat across my laced bra.

"You came here knowing exactly what this would be," he said, dragging his mouth along my jaw. "You wore this for me. Maybe you was hoping I'd ruin you."

167

My thighs squeezed together, but he pressed his leg in further, pinning me still.

"You want it rough, kotyonok?" he whispered, mouth at my ear. "You want to be manhandled? Owned? Fucked until you can't remember your own name?"

"Yes," I gasped, voice raw.

His grip on my throat pulsed—not cruel, just controlled. Just enough to make me feel it. Just enough to let me know he was everywhere.

"And you will be," he said darkly. "But not until you beg."

His hand slid down from my throat slowly, almost reverently, like he was unwrapping something precious—dangerous, sacred, his. The moment he released the pressure, I gasped, and he smiled like he'd won something.

Because he had.

"I want to hear it," he murmured, dragging his knuckles down my ribcage, stopping just above the waistband of my leggings. "Beg me."

I shivered, pulse thudding like a war drum.

"James..."

"That's not begging," he said flatly. "That's hesitation. You want this, kotyonok? Use your words."

My eyes fluttered closed. Every inch of me was burning—every nerve lit, every thought scrambled. All I could feel was him. His presence. His heat. His fucking control.

"Please," I whispered. "Touch me."

He rewarded me with a slow, sharp drag of his fingers beneath the waistband of my leggings, over my hips, possessive like he was carving his name into me.

"More," I breathed.

He chuckled darkly, leaning in until his mouth was a whisper against my ear. "You're soaked. All this attitude, all this resistance—and this is what you were hiding?"

He pushed my leggings and panties down in one smooth motion, letting them fall to the floor as he stepped back just enough to look at me—thoroughly, deliberately.

"Turn around," he said.

I hesitated. His eyes narrowed.

"Now."

I turned, bracing my hands against the wall again. My cheek pressed to the wood, breath shaky. I felt his hand slide up my spine, under my hoodie, over bare skin.

"I'm going to wreck you," he said, low and unrelenting.

I moaned, pushing back into his touch.

"Say it," he demanded.

"Wreck me," I whispered. "Please."

He didn't hesitate.

His hand wrapped back around my throat as he pressed into me from behind, his other hand dragging between my legs, teasing, taunting, ruining me inch by inch. I cried out, and he growled in approval.

"That's it," he muttered. "Louder."

He pressed his mouth to the back of my neck. "Mine," he growled. "All fucking mine."

And I was.

Every broken sound, every breathless gasp—I gave it to him willingly. Because in that moment, there was no one else.

30

Chapter 30

Lexi

I was already trembling when he pulled back, only to tear the rest of my clothes away like he couldn't bear the barrier between us a second longer. The air hit my skin, cool against heat, and then he was there again—behind me, wrapped around me, dragging the blunt head of his cock against me like a promise.

Then he paused.

"I'm taking you bare, kotyonok," he said, low. Controlled. Barely.

My breath caught. He knows I have an IUD but I have never had a man bare before.

Never done this before. No barriers. No safety net. Just skin to skin, consequence and commitment and something dangerously close to love.

"I want you like this," he said. "I want all of you. Every inch, every breath, every risk."

I turned my head, met his eyes.

"Yes," I whispered. "Take me like that."

And he did.

The first push was slow—too slow. I whimpered, pushing back, desperate for more. He cursed, low and harsh, and snapped his hips forward, burying himself in me fully.

I shattered around him.

There was no gentleness, no hesitation. He moved like he needed to erase the space between us—like he needed to brand me from the inside out. One hand fisted in my hair, the other still at my throat, keeping me where he wanted me.

"Mine," he growled. "No one else gets to touch you. No one else gets to hear these sounds. Only me."

He fucked me like he meant it. Like he owned me. Every thrust deeper, harder, perfectly punishing. My hands braced on the wall shook, my moans breaking between panting breaths and sharp cries.

But it wasn't just rough.

It was intimate.

He whispered things in Russian I couldn't understand, pressed kisses to my shoulder between thrusts, muttered my name like a prayer and a curse all at once. I could feel how close he was. Not just physically—but emotionally. Like he was teetering on the edge of something he didn't let himself have.

And when I came—sharp, helpless, unravelling—he held me through it. Never slowed. Never let go.

Then he followed, hips grinding deep one last time, growling my name as he came inside me, raw and bare and unfiltered.

When it was over, he didn't move.

He wrapped his arms around me, forehead pressed to the back of my neck, both of us shaking.

"You ruin me," he said softly. "Every fucking time."

And still, he didn't let go.

He kissed the back of my neck—soft this time. Lingering. And something about that simple touch made my heart ache in a way that was far more dangerous than anything he'd just done to my body.

We lay there for another minute, tangled and warm, the room spinning a little slower now.

Then he murmured against my skin, "Get dressed."

I blinked, rolling over just enough to look at him. "What?"

He pushed up onto his elbows, hair mussed, jaw tight, eyes softer than usual. "Hot tub. Outside. You said it was entrapment—might as well use it."

"Wait. *You* want to go sit in the hot tub and look at stars?"

He shot me a look. "Don't push it."

I laughed, still breathless. "Wow. A whole post-sex stargazing moment? What's next, you cook me breakfast and tell me about your childhood trauma?"

James gave me a flat look. "You want the hot tub or not?"

I smirked. "Oh, I want it."

"Good. Ten minutes. Actually don't get dressed. No clothes allowed."

He stood up, unapologetically naked, and walked out of the room without a backward glance.

And yeah.

Maybe I was already half in love with him.

31

Chapter 31

Lexi

Ten minutes, he said.

It took me five just to find my legs.

I pulled one of the soft hotel-grade robes from the bathroom hook and slipped into it, heart still pounding like I'd run a marathon uphill with a blindfold on. My body felt wrung out, marked, *owned*—in the most intoxicating way.

James wasn't in the living room when I came out, but the sliding door to the deck was cracked open. Cool mountain air drifted in, mixing with the faint smell of pine and whatever cologne still clung to the couch.

I stepped outside.

And instantly forgot how to breathe.

The hot tub was already steaming, glowing faintly beneath the canopy of stars. The view stretched out below us— mountains silhouetted in moonlight, valley lights glittering like someone had thrown diamonds across the earth. But it wasn't the scenery that stole my breath.

It was him.

James.

Already in the water. Naked.

His arms stretched out along the edge, head tilted back, eyes half-lidded as if this was just another Tuesday. Like I hadn't just unraveled beneath him. Like I wasn't standing there in a robe, skin still flushed from the way he'd broken me open.

He looked over.

And smiled. *That* smile.

"Robes are against the rules," he said, voice low and lazy, like sin had a sound.

I raised an eyebrow. "You never said that."

"I just did."

I stood there for a beat, letting the night air tease against the hem of my robe. He didn't look away. Didn't even blink. His stare was a challenge.

So I loosened the tie.

Let the fabric fall.

And stepped into the tub.

The heat wrapped around me instantly, curling over my skin like a second mouth. I sank down across from him, arms stretched along the edge, mimicking his posture even though my heart was pounding loud enough to echo.

He didn't move toward me.

He didn't have to.

The way he looked at me—slow and possessive and absolutely feral—told me everything I needed to know.

"You're staring," I said, trying to sound unimpressed.

"I *always* stare," he replied, voice like gravel dipped in whiskey. "But right now? I'm trying to figure out how the fuck I'm supposed to keep my hands off you."

"Don't," I said.

His eyes burned hotter than the water.

He pushed off the edge and closed the space between us in two slow, deadly strokes. His hands settled on my knees under the water. Warm. Large. Unrelenting.

"You're trouble," he murmured.

"And you," I whispered back, "are dangerous."

"A perfect match then."

His hands slid up my thighs—slow, torturous—spreading me beneath the water. I gasped as he moved between my legs, lowering his mouth to my stomach.

"You don't know what you do to me," he whispered.

I shivered. Not from cold—but from heat.

"Every inch of you," he continued, his lips brushing across my ribs, "drives me out of my fucking mind."

His mouth moved higher. Slower. Kisses so soft they ached.

"Your skin..." A kiss. "Your neck..." Another. "Your lips..." A slow press of his mouth to mine, full of restrained hunger.

"I don't want soft right now," he said, voice ragged. "I want messy. I want loud. I want you coming on my fingers while you scream my name to the fucking trees."

My breath caught.

He dipped his head, biting softly at my neck. "Can you be good for me, kotyonok?"

"No."

His laugh was low and dark, curling over my skin like smoke. "Even better."

He slid two fingers inside me under the water, thrusting hard, deep, deliberate. I cried out, head falling back against the edge as pleasure slammed through me like a freight train.

"You're soaked," he growled. "You've been soaked for me since you walked out here."

"James—"

"I want you to come like this," he said, thumb circling my clit as his fingers thrust harder. "With the stars above you. My name in your mouth. And my hand inside you."

I clawed at the sides of the tub, body shaking, chest heaving as he pushed me closer and closer to the edge.

"Say it," he whispered. "Say you're mine."

"I'm yours," I gasped. "Fuck—I'm yours, James—"

That was all he needed.

He kissed me hard as I came, his mouth swallowing my cries, his fingers never stopping, dragging it out until I was panting, writhing, begging for mercy.

When he pulled back, I was boneless, trembling, wrecked.

And he wasn't done.

He lifted me effortlessly into his lap, water sloshing over the edge, his cock pressing against me with dangerous intent.

"I need to be inside you," he rasped. "Now."

I reached down, guided him, and sank onto him in one slick, perfect slide.

We both groaned.

It was heaven.

His hands gripped my ass, guiding my rhythm as I rode him slow and deep, the water lapping around us like a heartbeat.

The stars above. His mouth at my throat. His hands everywhere.

It was everything.

And when we both came—together, again—it was stars behind my eyes and his name on my lips and the kind of ruin you never recover from.

We stayed like that for a long time—his arms around me, my cheek resting against his shoulder, the heat from the water mingling with the warmth I felt just being near him.

It was quiet out here. The kind of quiet that makes you feel like time has stopped. Like there's no past. No future. Just this.

Then, just as I was starting to feel myself drift, he whispered something low in Russian against the curve of my neck. Soft and reverent. Like a secret he didn't want the world to hear.

I froze.

"...What did you just say?"

He didn't answer right away. Just kept holding me, like if he let go, the night might disappear.

When he finally looked at me, his expression was unreadable—but his eyes, they were *bare*. Open. A little scared.

"Вы – это момент. Тот, кого хочется помнить, даже когда все остальное уже ушло. Я люблю тебя, котёнок."

My heart skipped so violently I thought it might stop.

I stared at him, stunned. "What does that mean?"

He brushed a damp strand of hair from my face, his fingers lingering on my cheek.

"One day," he said quietly. "But not tonight."

I opened my mouth to press him, to *ask*, but then he kissed my forehead—so gently, it almost broke me—and I couldn't.

Because whatever he'd said, I already felt it.

In the way he held me.

In the way he looked at me.

In the way I already knew... I was falling for him.

32

Chapter 32

Lexi

Eventually, James stirred beside me. A soft groan, a stretch, the kind of slow, predatory movement that made me painfully aware of every inch of him. Muscles shifting beneath skin, hair a little wild, jaw shadowed from sleep and sin. Dangerous in daylight. Still devastating.

"Morning," he rasped, voice rough and low, like it hadn't been used for anything but moaning the night before.

"Morning," I whispered, smiling into the pillow.

He didn't say anything for a moment—just looked at me. Really looked. Like he was still trying to figure out if I was real. Then he leaned over and kissed my shoulder—just once—like it was a habit he hadn't admitted yet.

When he pulled away, I already missed him.

He sat up and rolled out of bed in one fluid motion. Stretching, shirtless, unconcerned with my very obvious ogling. He reached for his jeans without hurrying, and it took everything in me not to drag him back into bed.

"Get dressed," he said, voice casual but commanding, already walking toward the bathroom.

I blinked. "Why do I feel like I'm about to be kidnapped again?"

He paused at the doorway and turned to look at me, smirking like he already had plans I couldn't handle. "You're about to have the best morning of your life." A beat. "Trust me."

I sat up, sheets sliding down my body, and caught the way his eyes flicked down—just for a second. Controlled. Calculated. But hungry.

"Is that a threat or a promise?" I asked, stretching like I wasn't still sore in the best way.

"Both," he said. "But only one of us is wearing underwear right now, so maybe don't test me."

I choked on a laugh and tossed a pillow at him. He dodged it effortlessly, still smug.

"You gonna tell me where we're going?" I called as he disappeared into the bathroom.

"Nope."

"Is it murder?"

"Not unless you keep asking questions."

I rolled my eyes and stood, moving slowly, pulling on yesterday's clothes because apparently mystery dates didn't come with wardrobe options. My body still hummed from the night before—sore in all the right places, skin marked in places no one else would see. And the worst part? I felt safe like this. Unguarded. Claimed.

By the time he reappeared, damp hair pushed back and smelling like my new addiction, I was dressed and leaning against the bed frame with my arms crossed.

"Well?" I said.

He walked straight to me. No hesitation. His hand curled around my jaw, thumb brushing my bottom lip.

"I think you might fall in love with me today," he murmured.

My heart did something reckless. Something I'd have to deal with later.

"You're awfully sure of yourself."

He smirked. Kissed me once. Slow. Certain.

"No, baby," he said. "I'm sure of *you*."

* * *

Twenty minutes later, I was bundled in a hoodie and boots, trailing James down a narrow, pine-scented path behind the cabin. The ground was still damp with dew, birds chirping far too cheerfully for how little sleep I'd gotten.

"Are we hiking toward something specific or is this just part of your ongoing plan to humble me with nature?" I asked, stepping over a root like it personally offended me.

"It's not my fault you packed for a spa day and not light cardio."

"I packed emotionally, not logically. There's a difference."

He didn't even look back—just smirked like he was enjoying my struggle far too much.

"And for the record," I added, already short of breath because apparently flirting was cardio now, "your coffee was so strong I'm pretty sure I unlocked another dimension."

"You're welcome."

I sighed dramatically, dragging my boots through the dirt like I was starring in a tragic period piece.

"You know, this is the part in the movie where the city girl twists her ankle and dies dramatically in her hot mountain boyfriend's arms."

"One, I'm not your boyfriend." He glanced over his shoulder. "Two, you're far too stubborn to die quietly."

"Romance is alive and well, I see."

He kept walking, refusing to reveal the destination, which obviously meant I kept asking.

Just when I was about to start threatening to turn back and demand pancakes, the trail opened up into a wide clearing—and I stopped dead.

"Okay... what the actual hell."

There was a stable.

An actual stable.

With actual horses.

James turned to face me, looking entirely too pleased with himself, hands on his hips like a rugged lumberjack-centaur hybrid.

"Surprise."

I blinked. "You have horses?"

"I don't have horses," he said with a shrug. "My neighbor boards them here. I just... borrow them."

"Borrow?"

He waved a hand. "We have an arrangement. He owes me a favor. Or seven."

"Does that favor include liability insurance? Because I should not be allowed near anything with hooves and a nervous system."

He walked over to a chestnut gelding like he was the goddamn Horse Whisperer, patting it with the casual confidence of someone who'd probably tamed dragons in another life.

"Relax," he said. "You'll be fine. You're light. They barely feel it."

"Are you calling me scrawny?"

"I'm saying if you fall off, you'll bounce."

"Wow," I deadpanned. "Nothing makes a girl feel cherished like being compared to a super ball."

We saddled up—well, he did, I mostly stood around pretending to help—and before I knew it, I was on a horse named Peanut who clearly had no interest in tolerating my chaos.

We rode side by side through the valley, sunlight warming our backs, the trees arching high above us like something out of a storybook.

James sat tall and confident in the saddle, reins in one hand like he'd done this a thousand times. I, on the other hand, was doing my best impression of someone who wasn't about to slide off sideways into a patch of moss.

"You look very... natural," he said, his voice all dry amusement.

"I hate you."

"You said you'd ridden before."

"Yeah. A pony. At a birthday party. When I was six."

He laughed—an actual, full laugh that did terrible things to my ribcage.

"God, you're a menace."

"And you're a horse-thief-slash-hockey-coach-slash-nightclub-mogul." I squinted at him. "Are you secretly a prince too?"

"I do have a tiara collection," he deadpanned.

"You joke, but now I kind of want to see you in one."

"Get through this ride without falling off and I'll consider it."

We talked. We teased. We raced once—he won, obviously—and when he reached down to help me dismount afterward, I pretended not to melt under the heat of his hands at my waist.

By the time we got back to the cabin, my cheeks hurt from smiling. My thighs hurt from Peanut. And my heart hurt just a little—because this? This kind of happiness? It was the kind you wanted to keep.

Even if you knew it wasn't built to last.

* * *

That evening, the smell of garlic and roasted herbs drifted from the kitchen while I changed into something soft and oversized, my hair twisted into a loose bun that I knew was halfway falling apart. My skin was still warm from the bath. My muscles loose. My heart... not so much.

When I stepped onto the balcony, I stopped cold.

A table for two.

Candles flickering, glasses already set, the lake in the distance catching the last blush of sunset like it was holding its breath. The air had cooled, but not enough to bite—just enough to make the flames dance in their holders, casting gold across the deck.

"You cooked?" I said, stepping into the light like it was a dream I wasn't sure I was allowed to have.

James turned, drying his hands on a towel, wearing a fitted black t-shirt that should've been outlawed in at least six countries. His hair was damp, pushed back. His expression soft, unreadable.

"I warned you," he said. "I'm good at a lot of things."

"Like being infuriating?"

"Like making a woman forget every red flag she ever saw."

I sat down, heart full, cheeks warm. "If this is some elaborate ploy to make me fall in love with you..."

He smirked as he poured the wine. "Is it working?"

Too well.

We ate by candlelight, the food somehow both simple and decadent. He'd made some kind of roasted chicken that tasted like magic and swore up and down it was just lemon and rosemary. I didn't believe him, but I let him have it.

We didn't talk about the team. Or Ethan. Or the fact that this could all crash and burn the moment we stepped back into real life.

We just... talked.

About food. About the cities we wanted to visit. About his terrible French and my tragic attempts to learn Russian.

"Say it again," he said, grinning. "One more time."

"It's not even a real word. You're making it up."

"It is. Say it."

I tried—and butchered it. Again.

Wine nearly came out of my nose as I laughed, choking and swatting at his smug expression.

"You're the worst teacher," I gasped. "That's not how you motivate students."

"You're the worst student," he countered. "No one's ever made 'delicious' sound like a threat before."

The sun dipped below the horizon, and the pink bled into indigo. The candlelight glowed against his jaw, and for a moment—just one—I let myself forget everything.

No fear. No future. Just this.

The weight of his gaze. The curve of his smirk. The way his thumb brushed the rim of his wine glass like he couldn't stop touching something.

When the meal ended, he didn't clear the table right away.

Just leaned back in his chair, watching me.

"You always get like this after dinner?" he asked, voice low.

"Like what?"

"Soft. Quiet." His eyes flicked to my mouth. "Ruinable."

My breath caught.

I looked away, pretending to focus on the moonrise.

Because it was perfect.

Too perfect.

And I knew the moment we left this place, everything would get complicated again.

But right now?

Right now, I let myself have it. The food. The heat. Him.

Because every so often, life gives you a moment that feels like a memory before it's even over.

And I wanted to remember this.

His voice. My laugh. The way the night wrapped around us like it knew we were running out of time.

* * *

After dinner, I offered to help clean up.

James just waved me off with a mock-stern look and a pointed dish towel.

"I cooked. You go enjoy the stars. I'll find you."

There was something sweet in the way he said it—casual, but full of promise. Like he didn't just mean *tonight*, but tomorrow too. And the day after that.

So I slipped away from the soft glow of the balcony and wandered barefoot down the lawn, a soft blanket draped over my shoulder. The earth was cool beneath my feet, dew-damp and smelling like pine and leftover warmth from the day.

The sky above was a cathedral of stars—endless, glittering, unbothered by anything that existed below.

I found a spot near the edge of the trees and spread the blanket out, then lay down with my hands folded over my stomach, letting the quiet settle around me.

Crickets hummed somewhere in the brush. The lake shimmered in the moonlight. My skin still buzzed from the day—his hands, his laughter, the kind of teasing that somehow felt like care in disguise.

I closed my eyes, just for a second.

I didn't hear him approach.

But then his shadow blocked the stars, and I opened my eyes to find him standing over me, moonlight painting the angles of his face, dish towel forgotten and probably dropped somewhere along the way.

"Room for one more?" he asked, voice lower now. Quieter.

"Always."

He dropped down beside me, warm and solid, the grass rustling beneath his weight. We lay there in silence, side by side, the blanket just big enough to keep us close. His shoulder brushed mine. Our legs barely touched. But it was enough to feel tethered.

Neither of us spoke.

We didn't have to.

The silence wasn't heavy. It wasn't awkward. It felt like a secret we both knew how to keep.

Then I felt it—his fingers brushing against mine. Soft. Tentative. Like he was asking permission he didn't need.

I turned my head toward him, and his eyes were already on me.

No smirk. No games. Just that look.

Quiet. Intense. Completely unguarded.

He reached out and tucked a loose strand of hair behind my ear, letting his fingers linger on my cheek like he wasn't quite ready to stop touching me.

"You make this feel easy," he said, almost like he didn't mean to say it out loud.

I blinked. "What?"

"Being here. With someone." He hesitated, exhaling slow. "I haven't felt that in a long time."

The words hit like gravity.

I didn't have anything clever to say. Nothing that would make it lighter. So I did the only thing that felt true.

I leaned in and kissed him.

Slow. Gentle. Not to ignite—but to keep.

His lips moved over mine like he was memorizing. One hand found the back of my neck. The other settled on my waist. He kissed me like we had time, like we were safe. Like maybe the world wouldn't fall apart when the sun came up.

And it wasn't about heat this time.

It was about everything else.

Softness. Trust. That slow-blooming ache that comes when you realize the person in front of you could ruin you simply by *leaving*.

We kissed like that for what felt like hours—under the stars, under everything. The kind of kiss that rewrites timelines. The kind that starts quietly but echoes forever.

Eventually, we pulled apart, breath shallow and mouths close.

He pressed his forehead to mine and whispered something in Russian.

"Ты меня спасаешь, даже не зная этого."

I smiled. "Okay, now that definitely sounds like emotional damage in Russian."

He laughed, quiet and warm. Kissed the tip of my nose like it was the most natural thing in the world.

We didn't say anything else.

We didn't need to.

Because for the first time, it didn't feel forbidden.

It just felt like love.

33

Chapter 33

Lexi

The smell of coffee was what woke me.

That, and the sound of someone humming—a low, slightly off-key hum that somehow made the luxury cabin feel like home. I blinked against the morning light, stretching beneath the soft sheets and immediately wincing at the *every-muscle-in-my-body-is-sore-in-the-best-way* kind of ache.

James Volkov: certified menace.

I sat up slowly, pulling the blanket with me, and padded into the kitchen wearing nothing but one of his t-shirts and the most satisfied expression known to mankind.

He was at the stove, barefoot, mug in one hand, flipping something in a skillet with the other like this was his full-time profession. His hair was damp from a shower, pushed back just enough to reveal the clean line of his jaw, and his voice was still hoarse when he spoke without turning around.

"You're late."

"For what? The post-coital farm chores?"

"Breakfast."

"Oh, *now* you're domestic?" I crossed my arms and leaned against the counter. "Should I start calling you Chef Daddy?"

He paused mid-flip.

Mid. Flip.

Then turned slowly, one brow arched, like he was mentally filing that phrase under "dangerous information to weaponize later."

"You want to say that again?" he asked, voice low and sharp with amusement.

I smirked. "I said *Chef Daddy*, too much for you to handle is it?"

His eyes narrowed. "You know I could *still* throw you over this counter, right?"

I tilted my head. "But would you pull your back?"

He stepped toward me, slow and deliberate, like a predator on a nature show. I held my ground—barely—because my legs were remembering *exactly* what happened the last time he got that look in his eye.

"You're playing a dangerous game, kotyonok."

"Yeah, but you like it."

He kissed me—quick, possessive, a little dirty for a kitchen— and then turned back to the stove like *he hadn't just short-circuited my entire nervous system.*

I exhaled. "Unfair."

He shrugged. "You started it."

I slipped into one of the stools at the counter, watching as he plated eggs, toast, and what appeared to be some suspiciously perfect bacon. "Is this real food or did you order room service to your fancy mountain hideaway?"

He slid the plate toward me. "Taste it and find out."

I did.

"Okay," I said with a mouthful. "Rude that you're hot *and* can cook."

"I also know how to field-dress a wound and build a fire from scratch."

I stared. "Are you just... stockpiling skills in case the apocalypse happens?"

"No," he said, sipping his coffee. "But if it does, you're definitely not surviving without me."

"Excuse you. I bring valuable talents."

He raised a brow. "Such as?"

"Sarcasm. Great hair. Excellent judgment in sweatpants."

He choked on his coffee.

I beamed.

We ate like that—bantering, flirting, pretending the clock wasn't ticking. Pretending the bags by the door didn't mean the real world was about to crash back in. His phone buzzed once from the counter. Mine buzzed twice. I didn't look.

James stood first, stretching slightly, and I had to bite my lip because that damn t-shirt was doing *unspeakable* things on his frame.

"Time to go," he said.

"Already?"

"Unless you want to miss the team meeting and let the media know we were both conveniently unavailable."

I sighed dramatically. "Fine. But I'm stealing your hoodie."

"I was going to offer it," he said, tossing it at me, "but now I'm going to bill you for it."

"You're lucky I didn't take the *cabin*, Volkov."

He grinned. "You *are* the most dangerous thing I've brought up here."

I pulled the hoodie over my head, his scent wrapping around me like an entire mood. "I'm flattered."

He didn't say anything else. Just looked at me—really looked—like he was taking inventory of every second we'd spent here and locking it away somewhere safe.

I pretended not to notice.

Because this wasn't supposed to *mean* anything.

It was just a reset. A break. A way to burn it out of our systems.

Right?

So why did leaving feel like cutting something real off at the root?

He held the door open as I stepped outside, the cool mountain air biting at my legs. I paused on the porch, staring at the view one last time.

James came up behind me, his chest brushing my back, and murmured, "You can come back whenever you want."

I turned. "I'll remember that."

He smirked.

I didn't kiss him again.

I wanted to.

God, I *wanted* to.

But if I did, I wasn't sure I'd be able to stop.

So I followed him to the car.

And we drove away in silence.

Back to the city.

Back to the team.

Back to the line we kept crossing, over and over again, like it was never really there in the first place.

34

Chapter 34

James

She kicked her feet up on the dash like she paid the insurance on this car.

Wearing nothing but my hoodie, her bare legs tucked up, hair a mess, sipping her overpriced oat milk latte like I hadn't just wrecked her in every room of that cabin—and the hot tub.

"You're going to get pulled over," I muttered, glancing at her knees.

"Why? For being too hot? That's not a real law."

"It is when it's distracting the driver."

She smirked and took another sip. "You like being distracted, Volkov."

I didn't answer.

Didn't have to. My silence was already screaming.

She stretched out like a cat, fingers dragging lazily across the center console like she was bored. Like she wasn't the most dangerous thing I'd ever let into my life.

"So, is this where we pretend we're not going back to a world that would implode if anyone saw us like this?" she asked.

"Pretending is your thing," I said, eyes still on the road. "I just survive it."

"Oh, come on," she grinned. "You loved that little fantasy weekend. Don't lie. You're practically glowing."

"Glowing?" I shot her a look. "Are you having a stroke?"

"Just saying. You cooked. You cuddled. You said emotionally confusing things in Russian. Very boyfriend-coded behavior."

"Lexi."

"Yes, Daddy?"

My hands tightened on the wheel.

She knew exactly what she was doing. And the smug little tilt of her mouth made it worse.

"Keep pushing," I said, voice low. "We'll be pulling over in the next ten miles, and you'll be walking home with that attitude."

"Sure, if I can walk at all," she said sweetly, eyes glittering with mischief.

Fucking hell.

I should've never taken her up there. Should've kept it clean. Clinical. Uncomplicated.

But nothing about Lexi Michelson was uncomplicated.

And control?

That was already a distant memory.

We drove in silence for a while, the mountains fading behind us in the mirror.

She picked the playlist.

Boybands. Luke Combs. A Taylor Swift track I had to white-knuckle my way through like a hostage in a getaway car.

And still—I couldn't stop the corner of my mouth from pulling up.

Because this girl? She was trouble.

And I'd never wanted anything more in my life.

35

Chapter 35

Lexi

I woke up feeling like I'd been hit by a truck made of sex, secrets, and ill-advised emotional vulnerability.

My body ached in a way that had nothing to do with soreness and everything to do with memory. The kind of ache that curled under your ribs and whispered: *you're in trouble*—but made you smile anyway.

Trouble had a name.

And it was James Volkov.

I was mid-sip of my coffee, trying to shake the night from my skin, when Rachel let herself in like the feral housemate she was—wearing sunglasses indoors and carrying an iced matcha like she was recovering from Coachella.

She didn't say hello.

She beelined for my closet, started pulling clothes off hangers with the focus of a stylist dressing a disaster and then flopped dramatically onto my bed.

"Tell me everything," she demanded.

"I already did."

"You gave me the bones. I want the flesh."

"Ew."

She ignored me, holding up a pair of jeans I hadn't worn since Obama's second term. "What exactly were you wearing when you emotionally bonded under the stars with your morally-compromised situationship?"

"I don't know. A blanket and a bad idea."

Rachel's eyes gleamed. "So... did he confess his darkest secrets? Did you cry? Did the moonlight make you say something poetic and humiliating?"

"No crying." I paused. "Some whispering. Mostly in Russian."

"Oh my god." She fell backward onto the bed like she'd just been personally blessed. "Did he say something cryptic that you'll Google at midnight and cry about in a week?"

I chucked a sweater at her face. "He's not a tragic poem in human form. He's just... complicated."

"Lexi." She lowered her sunglasses to look at me properly. "You slept with your ex's dad under the stars. That's not complicated. That's Greek mythology."

I groaned into my mug. "I'm going to work."

"I'll come." She sat up, already shoving her feet into sneakers she hadn't untied. "I can whisper my commentary into your earpiece like a deranged sports commentator."

"Absolutely not."

"Too late. I'm already emotionally invested."

I grabbed my bag and started toward the door.

"You know this ends in chaos, right?" she called after me.

I paused. Glanced over my shoulder. "Yeah," I said. "But it's starting in something kind of beautiful."

Rachel blinked. Then grinned.

"You're so screwed."

"I know."

And I smiled anyway.

* * *

Game day energy was already buzzing through the stadium when we arrived.

The comms crew was hyped. Camera batteries charging, mic packs blinking like tiny bombs of chaos, interns running like caffeinated ducklings. I slid into gear like muscle memory—clipboard in hand, camera strap across my chest, smile locked and loaded.

The team was already in full clown mode.

Connor had his jersey half-on, yelling at Ryan about who stole his protein bar like it was a federal crime. Ryan, holding said protein bar, was eating it with aggressive eye contact.

Liam, shirtless and holding a whiteboard marker, was narrating everything like a hyperactive wildlife documentary.

"And here we have the lesser-spotted defenseman, typically passive until you touch his snacks. Watch how he bares his teeth. Majestic."

"I will fight you," Connor grumbled, pulling his jersey over his head.

"I hope you do. My cardio needs a purpose."

Even Ethan looked relaxed, leaning against the bench and joking with one of the trainers, his expression lighter than I'd seen it in weeks. The grin was back—the one that used to get him out of PR disasters. It didn't reach all the way to his eyes, but it was close.

It felt like something healing.

"You're late," Ethan called when I walked in.

"You're lucky I showed up at all," I shot back, sidestepping an intern and adjusting my camera strap.

"Ooh, she's got attitude today," Ryan chimed in, grinning like a demon. "Someone must've had a good weekend."

I ignored him, lifted my camera, and snapped a picture of him mid-smirk.

"Too close," he said, blinking.

"Too late," I replied. "Your pores are public now."

Laughter echoed behind me as I moved through the chaos, catching content for socials. Skate tap routines. Slow-mo shots of tape wrapping around sticks. Mic'd-up moments I'd later have to censor.

Connor posed dramatically with his stick like he was about to duel the ghost of Wayne Gretzky.

"Lexi, get my good side."

"You don't have one."

"Rude!"

I turned, still laughing—and froze.

James.

Black suit. Sleeves rolled. Arms crossed.

Watching the room like he wasn't trying to set fire to my circulatory system.

I raised the camera slowly, pretending to adjust my ISO.

He didn't move.

I zoomed in. He smirked. Just a little.

Snap.

"Filming the coach now?" Ethan's voice appeared at my shoulder, casual but sharp. "Is that what we're doing?"

I turned. "Everyone's fair game."

He raised an eyebrow but didn't push it.

"He's not going viral unless you catch him yelling at a ref or power-walking aggressively through a hallway."

"Noted." I said, forcing calm, ignoring the fact that James was still watching.

Still smirking.

So I lifted the camera again.

James leaned forward slightly. Just enough for me to notice.

"Got something to say?" I muttered, framing the shot.

"Just wondering if your camera's waterproof," he said, eyes flicking to my mouth. "Because you keep looking at me like that, I might do something about it."

I didn't blink.

Click.

"Smile for the fans, Coach."

His gaze was sharp enough to cut through kevlar.

"Don't test me in my own locker room, kotyonok."

"You're the one playing with fire."

He didn't smile. But he didn't look away either.

And just like that—I was back in the cabin. Naked. Breathless. Ruined.

My hands clenched around the camera like it might save me from myself.

Spoiler: it wouldn't.

"You okay?" Rachel appeared beside me with the energy of someone who'd already had three espressos and was high on drama.

"Fine." I said tightly.

"Uh huh." She followed my line of sight. "Well, if it's any consolation, you're not the only one staring. That man is undressing you with his eyes like it's his actual job."

"Please stop."

"I will never stop."

We both looked over toward Ethan, who was now laughing with Liam and actually... smiling. For real. No edge. No shadows.

"It's nice seeing him like this again," Rachel said quietly, nudging my arm. "Feels like old times. Except, you know, better."

And she wasn't wrong.

For a moment, it really did feel epic.

The whole room was buzzing with energy—not just game day adrenaline, but something bigger. Like we were all part of a story that hadn't reached its climax yet. A pause before the plunge.

The guys were loud, confident, chaotic in the best way. Liam threw a roll of tape across the locker room and Connor caught it behind his back without blinking.

"Okay, that was hot," Rachel muttered. "Don't tell him I said that."

"Oh, I'm absolutely telling him."

"Lexi, I swear—"

The buzzer sounded overhead—final call for warmups. The room shifted, snapping into focus. Players grabbed sticks, helmets, gloves. Coaches started barking orders. The air thickened with intention.

James caught my eye one last time before walking out.

And I knew. The second this game ended, everything between us was going to boil over again.

Because the only thing more dangerous than playing with fire?

Was pretending you wouldn't get burned.

36

Chapter 36

Lexi

We'd just settled into our usual spot by the bench, camera in hand, crowd roaring in that electric, goosebump-inducing way that only comes with home games. My lens was steady, tracking the puck drop like it was instinct, not muscle memory. Focused. Professional. In the zone.

And then—

"Hey, sweetheart!"

The voice cut through the sound like a blade. Loud. Drawling. Laced with that specific brand of lazy, performative testosterone that thrived in away-game locker rooms and locker room TikToks.

I didn't flinch. Didn't look. I'd heard worse.

"You that team media girl?" he kept going. Too loud. Too confident. The kind of guy who still called women 'baby girl' and thought finger guns were foreplay.

Still didn't look.

"Damn, you're hot. Come take my picture after the game—

I'll make it worth your while."

There were a few chuckles from his bench. Nothing loud. Just enough to say *we've all seen him do this before, and none of us are going to stop him.*

I kept filming. Eyes glued to the viewfinder. Jaw tight.

"I'd love to see what else you could shoot," he added, voice dipping just enough to make my skin crawl. "Bet you'd look fuckable holding something else in your hands." A slow, exaggerated whistle. "Fuuuuck."

My grip slipped.

Just for a second.

And I turned.

Number 91. Opposing team. Leaning too far over the boards, helmet cocked to the side, mouthguard half-hanging like he thought it was charming. He gave me a wink that felt like an infection. And then a slow, two-fingered kiss blown in my direction.

Like I was decoration.

Like I was his.

But I wasn't the only one who heard it.

To my left, James went completely still.

Utterly still.

Like every muscle in his body snapped taut in perfect, deadly silence. His hand, resting on the bench edge, curled into a fist. One breath. Two.

The air around him dropped ten degrees.

He didn't move.

But I saw it—his nostrils flare. His jaw twitch. His temple pulse.

I put a hand on his forearm.

Not to stop him. Just to remind him—I'm here. I've got this.

203

He didn't look at me.

His eyes were locked on Number 91 like he was mentally measuring how many bones he could break before security intervened.

"Ignore him," I muttered under my breath. "He's trying to get a reaction."

James didn't answer.

But he smiled.

Slow. Dark. Razor-sharp.

And whispered, just loud enough for me to hear:

"I'll give him one, if he comes near you again."

* * *

The game rolled on, but the energy had shifted—sharp and volatile, like static before lightning. Every second on the clock felt like a warning. My hands gripped the camera, but I wasn't filming. Not really. My heart was pounding too hard, drowning out the noise, the movement, the play.

I tracked Number 91 every time he hit the ice. Watched the way he skated too close to the bench, too slow. Like he was circling prey. Like he was looking for something.

Then came the stoppage.

And he skated past again—smug, swaggering, like he owned the air around him. This time, he reached. Gloved fingers out, just a little too casual, like he was going to brush my arm.

Or my hip.

Or maybe just prove that he *could.*

He didn't get the chance.

Because James Volkov detonated.

Off the bench.

Off the leash.

One second, I was staring at a smirk.

The next—*chaos.*

Number 91 hit the ice with a sickening *crack*, James on top of him like a force of nature—fists already flying. No gloves. No hesitation. Just raw, unleashed fury.

The first punch split skin.

The second drew blood.

By the third, Number 91's helmet had popped off and his nose was spraying crimson across the white ice like something biblical.

James was shouting in Russian. Low, guttural. Like the words were knives. The kind of rage that wasn't just about a game—it was personal. Old. Primal.

The crowd roared like animals.

The refs blew whistles hard enough to rupture lungs.

I just stood there.

Frozen.

Breath caught. Blood singing in my ears. My camera dangled at my side, forgotten.

The bench exploded.

Liam launched over the boards like a missile, gloves in the air, screaming something about respecting women before he tackled the nearest opponent. Carter was right behind him, swinging wild and grinning like he was having the time of his life.

Even Connor—sweet, banana-bread Connor—raised his stick like it was a goddamn sword and charged.

It wasn't a fight.

It was a fucking war.

Helmets clattered. Jerseys tore. A linesman got knocked on

his ass. Fans screamed like it was the Stanley Cup and *The Purge* rolled into one.

And through the mayhem, James never looked away from Number 91—still snarling, chest heaving, blood smeared across his face and fists. He stood like a soldier, like a storm, daring anyone to try him again.

"OFF THE ICE!" a ref bellowed, pointing like he was banishing a demon. "NOW!"

James didn't flinch.

Didn't argue.

He just turned and *stalked* toward the tunnel—rage radiating off him like heat, blood dripping from his knuckles, black suit jacket hanging torn off one shoulder like a villain in a final act showdown.

And then—

"What the hell was that?!"

Ethan.

He vaulted over the boards and hit the tunnel at full speed, skates slicing into the ice as he chased after James.

I followed—on instinct. On adrenaline. On the sheer need to know what the hell had just happened and if I was still breathing.

"That was over the line!" Ethan shouted, his voice bouncing off the hallway walls. "You don't get to pull that shit just because someone pissed you off!"

James didn't stop walking.

"Back off, Ethan," he growled, voice low and dangerous.

"You're supposed to be our *coach*, not a goddamn hitman—"

"I said *back off.*"

And the way James turned on him—slow, deliberate, eyes dark and teeth bared—was enough to make Ethan fall silent mid-stride. Just for a second.

I stayed frozen in the hallway, camera limp in my hands, lungs refusing to work.

Then Rachel appeared beside me, breathless, mascara slightly smudged, clutching a Red Bull like she'd sprinted through a battlefield.

"Tell me I did not just watch your man go full John Wick on the ice because someone got grabby."

I couldn't speak.

Because technically?

He wasn't my man.

But in that moment—watching him bleed for me, break for me, *burn* for me?

He had never felt more mine.

And that?

That was a problem.

A dangerous, violent, irreversible problem.

37

Chapter 37

James

I stormed down the tunnel, blood pounding in my ears louder than the crowd's roar. My vision tunneled. My pulse thundered. I didn't feel the sting in my knuckles, or the blood smeared across them. I didn't feel anything.

All I could hear was the sound of *his* voice—

You that team media girl?

—and the way Lexi flinched.

That was all it took.

She shouldn't have had to hear that. Shouldn't have had to *pretend* it didn't matter. And she sure as hell shouldn't have had to stand there while he reached for her like she was *available* for touching. For humiliating.

No.

No.

Not on my ice.

Footsteps pounded behind me, fast and furious. I didn't turn around. I didn't need to.

"Don't fucking walk away from me!"

Ethan's voice cracked like a whip, slicing through the echo of the crowd still buzzing above.

I exhaled once.

Calm. Controlled.

Barely.

"Go cool off," I muttered. "This isn't the time."

He didn't listen.

Of course he didn't. He was my son. And angry.

"What the hell was that out there?!" he barked, coming up fast. "You just threw yourself at a guy *in the middle of the game.* You're the coach! Are you *trying* to get suspended?"

I stopped walking.

Turned. Slowly.

Let the full weight of my glare land on him like a sledgehammer.

"He put his hands on Lexi."

Ethan froze.

All that bluster—cut clean.

"What?"

"He said some shit. Crossed the line. Then he reached for her."

His brows furrowed.

Confused. Defensive. Ready to deflect—

And then it hit him.

Right there in the center of his face.

I watched it happen like slow-motion destruction.

The flicker of confusion.

The flash of realization.

The silence before the scream.

His jaw tensed.

Breath hitched.

And he backed up half a step like I'd just punched him in the gut.

"You... you and her?" he said, voice cracking. Disbelieving. Disgusted. "No. No fucking way."

I didn't answer.

Didn't need to.

He already knew.

"Are you *serious?*" His voice hitched higher. Louder. "*Lexi?* She's my ex, man! That's who you've been sneaking around with? The girl I used to—"

"Don't," I snapped. Sharp. Dangerous. "Don't finish that sentence."

His laugh was ugly.

Bitter and young.

"Wow. *Un-fucking-believable.* You ditch me for twenty goddamn years, and when you finally show up—you fuck the one girl I ever—"

"Lexi wasn't a plan," I bit out. "She wasn't some scheme. She happened."

"That's your defense?" he spat. "That it *happened?* Jesus Christ—how long?"

I stepped forward. Slowly.

"It started before we knew."

He blinked.

"What?"

"She was just a girl in a bar. And I was... just a man. We didn't know. Not at first."

He stared at me, like trying to find the lie.

Then—

"And after?"

Silence.

That was all the answer he needed.

His voice dropped to a whisper.

"You *kept going.* Even after you knew."

I nodded once.

Sharp. Cold. Honest.

"I tried to stop," I said quietly.

That was the wrong thing to say.

His laugh this time—

Wasn't bitter.

It was *broken.*

"You *tried?*"

He took a step forward and *shoved me*—hard—straight in the chest.

"You tried?! That's what I get? That's your grand apology for fucking my ex-girlfriend and ruining the one thing we could've fixed?!"

I didn't move.

Didn't hit back.

Didn't defend myself.

I let him hit.

Let him burn.

"I needed you when I was five," he said, voice cracking into something that barely sounded like rage anymore. "Not now. And *not like this.*"

My chest twisted.

"I know," I said.

And I *meant it.*

But it wasn't enough.

Not even close.

He shoved past me, storming toward the locker room doors,

skates echoing like gunshots against the concrete.

I didn't follow.

I stood there.

Alone.

In the wreckage.

In the blood on my hands and the silence I built for two decades.

And the worst part?

We lost the game.

By two goals.

First loss of the season.

But that wasn't the part that mattered.

Because I didn't just lose a game.

I lost my son.

Again.

And this time—

It was *all* my fault.

38

Chapter 38

Lexi

I didn't even stay for the end of the game.

I couldn't.

Not after what I saw—Ethan storming after James down the tunnel, his voice raised, his face twisted in a way I'd never seen before. Like something had finally snapped. Like all the threads we'd been desperately pretending weren't tangled just *ripped* apart in one violent pull.

And God... he knew.

He *knew*.

I barely made it to my car before the tears started.

Not the pretty, single-tear kind. These were the breathless, hot, choking kind. The kind that didn't even ask permission. The kind that wrecked your makeup, your pulse, your soul.

I drove.

I didn't know where. I didn't care. I just needed to *move*. To get away from the arena, the lights, the cameras, the thousands of people who had no idea what they'd just witnessed. Or worse—who *did.*

By the time I got home, my body was shaking.

I dropped my bag just inside the door, kicked off my shoes like they were made of glass, and collapsed onto the couch like gravity had finally stopped pretending it wasn't trying to bury me alive. My chest felt like it had been scooped out. Hollow. Raw.

And then the door opened.

"Lexi?"

Rachel.

And behind her—Maya.

Of course they came. Of course they knew.

I didn't ask how. I didn't *need* to. They were my people. The kind of women who didn't wait to be called when the house was on fire. They just kicked the damn door in.

Rachel scanned the room once and dropped her bag like it was an emergency. "Okay. Blankets. Wine. Emergency chocolate. Possibly crime scene cleanup if necessary. Maya, get the playlist. I want the sad bitch anthems."

I tried to laugh, but it came out like a wheeze.

Maya didn't say anything. She just crossed the room, curled onto the couch beside me, and wrapped an arm around my shoulders. Her warmth hit me like a match to dry kindling.

That was when I cracked open.

My head dropped to her shoulder, and I cried. Not the silent kind. Not anymore. These were ugly, trembling, *ripping* sobs. The kind that pulled up everything I'd been holding back for weeks. Months.

It wasn't just heartbreak. It wasn't just fear. It was shame. Regret. The grief of something *almost* beautiful turning to ash in your hands.

Rachel reappeared with two glasses of wine, a pint of ice cream, and her hair already twisted into a bun like she was preparing for emotional combat.

"What happened?" she asked gently, crouching down in front of me.

I wiped my nose with the sleeve of James's hoodie—still oversized, still warm, still smelling like something I *wasn't allowed to want.*

"He knows."

Maya rubbed my back softly. "Ethan?"

I nodded, my throat tight. "He heard James say something. Or enough to *know.* I saw it land on his face like a goddamn bomb."

Rachel winced. "Shit."

"Yup."

"What did he do?" Maya asked softly.

"I don't know," I whispered. "I didn't follow them. I couldn't. I just... I ran. I couldn't watch it. I couldn't be there when it broke."

Silence followed that. The kind that's heavy. Full of things no one wants to say.

Then Rachel leaned in and brushed my hair behind my ear. "Are you okay?"

"No." The word cracked open my throat like glass. "He looked at James like he hated him. And I—" My voice broke again. "I *know* I don't get to be heartbroken over that. But I am."

"You're not heartless," Rachel said quietly. "You're just human. You didn't do this to hurt anyone."

"Doesn't matter," I said. "I still did. I *hurt* him. And James... I don't even know if he's okay. Ethan went after him like he

215

wanted to fight. Like it all just... snapped."

Maya's hand tightened around mine. "Do you think he'll come here?"

I shook my head. "He wouldn't. Not with Ethan like that. Not when everything's bleeding out all over the floor."

Rachel curled up on the armrest and sighed like it physically hurt. "Okay. So we do what we always do."

"Which is?"

"Step one: remind you that you are not the villain in this story."

Maya nodded. "Step two: accept that everything is a shit-show and it's okay to lie face-down on the floor about it."

"And step three," Rachel added, raising her wine glass, "we hold the line. We survive it together. Until the next chapter."

I stared at them—at these beautiful, loud, emotionally reckless women who had seen me through everything.

And something inside me *shifted.*

The pain didn't leave.

But it *settled.*

Tucked in beside the love.

Because maybe this was it.

Maybe this was what survival looked like.

Bleeding. Bruised. Held together by messy bun energy and off-brand Chardonnay.

"What if I ruined everything?" I asked, quietly. Childishly. Like I was five years old again and afraid of the dark.

Maya looked me dead in the eye.

"Then we rebuild it. From the ashes. And this time? With better lighting."

I laughed. A real one.

It hurt.

But it was real.

And right now, that was enough.

Just this.

One breath.

One moment.

One night at a time.

39

Chapter 39

Lexi

I didn't even bother setting an alarm. I knew before I opened my eyes that I wasn't going in, again. Its been almost a week and two missed games. I called in sick again around 7:30 a.m., voice hoarse and shaky as I left a voicemail for HR, then dropped my phone on the nightstand and crawled back under the covers.

My stomach was twisted in knots, my head heavy with the echo of Ethan's voice, and my had been shattered.

I didn't sleep.

I just... hid.

Around 9:15, my phone buzzed. Once. Then again. Then a rapid-fire series of pings.

Groaning, I reached for it, blinking blearily at the screen.

[New Group Chat: "Team Chaos + One"]
    Liam: *Hey Lexi. Heard you were out today. Just checking in.*

Connor: *Are you alive? Blink twice if yes.*

Carter: *We voted and we're pretty sure yesterday broke you.*

Liam: *We also voted and decided it was* kind of *worth it.*

Connor: *Don't listen to him, he cried when he got benched.*

Carter: *Real talk tho—u good?*

I stared at the screen, stunned.

Then another message came in.

Liam: *Also... mad respect for landing the coach.*

Carter: *Yeah, like?? Damn girl.*

Connor: *I'd climb him like a tree and I don't even swing that way.*

Liam: *That man is* built *like a brick wall.*

Carter: *And angry. Like, angry-hot.*

Connor: *You okay tho? We're all team Lexi over here.*

Tears pricked my eyes again, but this time they weren't from heartbreak.

I laughed. Actually laughed.

Me: *You guys are ridiculous. Also I hate all of you. But thank you* ♥

Liam: *We love you too.*

Carter: *Don't ghost us. You miss one more game, and we're sending a rescue mission.*

Connor: *Or nudes. Either way.*

I set the phone down on my chest, smiling just a little. It didn't fix everything. It didn't erase the ache.

But it reminded me I wasn't alone.

And maybe—just maybe—I could face whatever came next.

Eventually.

* * *

I don't know how long I lay there after I put my phone down. The texts helped—God, they helped—but they didn't cure anything. They didn't unburn the bridge. They didn't unstitch my heart from where it had knotted itself around James Volkov.

By the time I heard the knock at the door, I'd already told myself it wasn't him.

Couldn't be him.

Except... it was.

I opened the door without thinking, like my body already knew who it would be before my brain caught up.

James stood there in the doorway, looking like a man who hadn't slept in a week. Dark jeans, plain t-shirt, a hoodie pulled halfway over his head like he hadn't decided if he was coming to stay or run the second I opened the door.

My breath caught in my throat.

His eyes met mine.

And just like that—I shattered.

"You look like hell," I said softly, because my hands were already shaking.

"So do you," he said. His voice was low, rough, like every word cost him something.

I stepped back to let him in.

He didn't move.

"I can't stay," he said quickly, like if he didn't say it fast, he'd break the rule he was about to lay down.

My stomach dropped.

"I talked to Ethan," he continued. "We've had... more than

a few conversations since that night."

I nodded slowly, heart already crumbling. "And?"

"And we agreed to try again," he said, eyes locking on mine. "Not to fix everything. But to at least stop destroying each other."

I couldn't speak. My throat was burning. My chest felt like it might cave in.

"There's one condition," he said, voice quieter now. "One thing he asked."

I already knew. I knew what was coming before the words left his mouth.

"That I stay away from you."

The silence was deafening. My body folded in on itself, trying to disappear under the weight of it.

"I didn't agree right away," he said, stepping just barely over the threshold. "I couldn't. Because it's you, Lexi. You're the only thing that's felt real in years."

Tears spilled over, hot and fast.

"But I owe him this," he said, swallowing hard. "I owe him a shot. At something—at anything. And I know you'd never want to be part of the reason that broke him any more than I already have."

I shook my head, wiping my face with the sleeve of the hoodie I hadn't taken off in days. "Of course not. I just... I thought maybe..."

"I know," he said, stepping closer now. "So did I."

We were face to face. Barely a breath apart. The ache between us wasn't just emotional—it was in my bones. In the hollowness of my chest. In the scream behind every heartbeat that wanted to tell him not to go.

He reached out, gently brushing a tear from my cheek.

"I never wanted to hurt you kotyonok," he said, voice raw. "If things were different…"

I stepped forward before I could stop myself, burying my face in his chest, gripping the hem of his hoodie like if I held on hard enough, it wouldn't end.

He held me back just as tight.

Neither of us spoke.

There was nothing left to say.

After a long minute, he tilted my chin up. His thumb traced the edge of my lip.

"One last kiss," he said, barely a whisper. "Just one."

I nodded.

He kissed me like he'd never get to again.

Because he wouldn't.

It was slow. Deep. Memorized. Like he was imprinting it. Like I was.

He pulled back and whispered against my lips, ''Я тебя люблю.''

And walked out the door.

I didn't close it.

I couldn't.

I stood there for a long time, heart in pieces on the floor, waiting for the ache to dull.

It didn't.

40

Chapter 40

James

Two weeks.

That's how long it had been since I told her I loved her.

Since I told her goodbye in the same breath.

I thought time would help. That staying busy, keeping my head down, focusing on the team—on Ethan—would dull the edge of it.

It hadn't.

It was just a quieter kind of hurt now. The ache that didn't scream anymore, but settled deep in your bones like winter.

I stepped onto the ice for morning training, the cold biting at my skin through my jacket. The players were already out there, tossing pucks, chirping each other, laughing like they were carrying none of the weight I was dragging behind me.

"Let's move, boys!" I barked, voice sharp. "Wheels on the line. Three rounds."

They groaned, but moved. Always did.

I paced behind the bench, clipboard in hand, calling drills

like it was muscle memory. Because it was. I knew how to run a team. Knew how to rebuild plays, fix a weak forecheck, pivot around a struggling defenseman.

What I didn't know how to do was stop seeing her in every damn corner of this rink.

She used to be here in the mornings. Camera slung over her shoulder, hair tucked in a ponytail, coffee in one hand, laughing at something Liam said.

Now?

I hadn't seen her in weeks.

Ethan had been... different. Less angry. More focused. He was talking to me again. Training harder. Giving me short, tight nods when I offered correction.

It should've felt like progress.

But all I could think was—*was it worth it*?

Was gaining a son worth losing the one person who made me feel like more than my mistakes?

"Hey, Coach!"

Liam skated past, flicking a puck behind him like it was nothing. "You gonna join us out here or just scowl from the bench all day?"

"Scowling's my specialty," I muttered, but I stepped onto the ice anyway, stick in hand.

Because for now, this was all I had.

The ice.

The team.

And the empty space where she used to be.

By the second hour on the ice, the drills had stopped being about training and started looking more like punishment.

"Again," I barked, voice echoing off the boards. "Harder

this time. If you're not gassed by the end of this round, you didn't do it right."

The players were bent over at the waist, sweat dripping, gloves tugged off and hanging from the ends of their sticks. But they didn't argue. They just skated. Harder. Faster.

Because they knew better.

No one pushed back when I got like this.

Not when I was in a mood. Not when I was like *this*.

Out of control in the most composed way.

"You good, Coach?" Connor asked, panting as he skated by.

"Skate," I snapped. "Talk later."

He nodded and kept moving.

I didn't even know what I was doing anymore—training or bleeding out. All I knew was I had to keep moving, keep barking orders, keep my feet on the ice or I'd fall through the cracks I'd made for myself.

"Line up!" I barked. "Let's go, again. You're moving like you've got cinder blocks for legs. Pick it up!"

Liam skated past, giving me a wary look. "Coach, we've done this drill six times."

"Then make the seventh count."

He didn't argue. Just nodded and dropped back in line.

The players knew.

They didn't say anything—but I could feel it.

The weight in their glances. The silent understanding.

They all knew what this was really about.

Even Ethan.

* * *

By the time I stepped off the ice, my voice was hoarse from shouting, my shoulders burning, and the boys looked like they'd just survived a military boot camp.

They didn't complain—at least, not to my face.

But the silence said enough.

Gear hit the floor harder than usual. Tape was ripped with more frustration than finesse. The air in the locker room was thick with sweat, steam, and something heavier.

I didn't say a word as I tugged off my jacket, undid the cuffs of my shirt, and unbuttoned it one-handed while walking to the showers. Just needed a minute. A second to breathe. To let the heat beat the thoughts out of my head.

The metal pipes groaned as I turned the water on full blast, steam rising immediately, fogging up the glass.

I stepped under the stream.

Let it scald.

It had been weeks.

Weeks of silence.

Of restraint.

Of doing the "right" thing—every single fucking day.

I kept my head down. Put Ethan first. Focused on the team. Played the part.

And still... it wasn't enough.

Every morning, I told myself the ache would dull.

Every night, I told myself I was doing the right thing.

And every time I closed my eyes, she was there.

I leaned forward, bracing both hands on the cold tile wall, head bowed under the punishing spray of the shower. Steam curled around me, but I couldn't get warm. Couldn't feel anything but the pressure building in my chest.

I missed her.

God, I *missed her.*

Not just the nights. Not just the heat of her body wrapped around mine or the way her voice hitched when I touched her just right.

I missed her *laugh.* That dry, reckless, from-the-gut sound that made something *human* in me twitch back to life.

I missed the way she *argued* with me. No fear. No hesitation.

I missed the quiet moments. Her curled up in a hoodie, bare feet on my dashboard, bitching about my coffee like it was a war crime.

I missed the way she looked at me.

Like I wasn't a mistake.

Like I wasn't just a name with stats and a past full of ash.

Like I was *someone.* Still worth the fight.

And I hated—*hated*—that doing the right thing meant walking away from the only person who'd ever made me feel like I had something left to give.

I punched the wall once.

Not hard enough to break anything. Just enough to *feel* something.

The water kept running.

Hot. Pointless.

And I stayed there—forehead against tile, eyes closed, jaw clenched so tight it ached—while the steam swirled around me like smoke from a life I'd already burned down.

She was everywhere.

In my bed.

In my ribs.

Under my fucking skin.

And the worst part?

The *right* thing didn't feel right anymore.
It just felt like *loss.*

41

Chapter 41

James

It had been a month.

Twenty-eight days of staying away from the one thing I couldn't stop wanting.

Lexi had disappeared for the first two. Out "sick," according to HR. But everyone knew what that meant.

She'd been shattered.

Gutted.

And I'd been the knife.

When she finally came back, she wasn't the same.

Still Lexi on paper—same sharp wit, same clipped professionalism, same immaculate execution.

But the spark? Gone.

She didn't wear the jerseys anymore.

Didn't chirp the players from behind the camera.

Didn't meet my eyes. Ever.

And me?

I coached like a machine. Ran drills. Made notes. Yelled in all the right places. But I was going through the motions. Because I'd made my choice.

Ethan.

My son.

The reason I'd walked away from the only thing that had made me feel alive in years.

And I'd do it again.

Because some things matter more than want. More than heat. More than aching skin and ruined bedsheets and whispered promises in the dark.

But damn if it didn't hurt.

Game day.

Final regular season game. Packed house. Playoff placement on the line. Everyone was dialed in.

Except me.

I spotted her the moment I stepped onto the ice.

Lexi. Across the arena. Head down, gear in hand, looking like she'd rather be anywhere else.

She hadn't missed as many games lately. But she wasn't really here either. She stayed behind the camera. Let others do the talking. Took on only what was necessary and nothing more.

And I let her.

Because I'd promised Ethan I'd stay away.

But it didn't mean I stopped seeing her. Feeling her. Every. Damn. Day.

The locker room buzzed with energy. Pre-game rituals. Stick tape, blasting music, last-minute shit talk.

But something was... off.

They all felt it. The shift. The space Lexi and I had left behind like an open wound no one wanted to poke too hard.

I was lacing up a clipboard of adjustments when Ethan approached me—quiet, grounded, a little older than he'd been a month ago.

"Hey," he said.

I looked up. "Yeah?"

He hesitated. Then sat beside me, elbows on his knees.

"I just wanted to say... thank you."

I blinked. "For what?"

"For... putting me first. For the last few weeks. For giving me space to figure shit out."

I stared at him. "You don't need to thank me for that, Ethan."

"I do," he said, more certain now. "You didn't owe me that. But you've shown up. For me. Even when it cost you everything."

The words hit harder than I expected.

I swallowed the lump in my throat. "I've made a lot of mistakes. But not showing up for you again wasn't going to be one of them."

He nodded slowly. "I know that now. And I didn't say it before, but... I'm glad you're here. Really here."

His voice cracked just a little on that last part.

I looked at my son—really looked at him—and felt something tighten in my chest.

Pride. Regret. Relief. Pain.

All of it.

"I'm proud of you," I said. "For how you've handled all this. You didn't have to."

He exhaled like he'd been holding something in for weeks. "It hasn't been easy. But... I get it now. Why it happened. Why you pulled back."

He looked down at his hands.

"I miss her too, you know. I understand how you could have fallen for her, like I did. She's an easy person to love."

That nearly undid me.

Before I could say a word, he stood and clapped me on the shoulder.

"Let's go win this thing," he said.

And just like that, he was gone. Back to his locker. Back to his team.

And I sat there, floored by the kid who'd somehow turned into a man right in front of me.

Ten minutes later, I stepped onto the bench.

Lexi was across the ice again. Still not looking at me. Still wearing that same guarded expression.

But I didn't need her eyes to know she was hurting.

Because I was hurting too.

And somehow... that felt like the only thing we still shared.

42

Chapter 42

James

The horn blew.

Loud. Deafening. Final.

Win.

The arena exploded.

Crowd on their feet, players tossing gloves into the air, slamming sticks into the boards in celebration. Music thumped through the speakers—something loud and victorious—but it was nothing compared to the sound of this locker room.

Laughter. Yelling. Pure chaos.

It was the final game of the regular season—and we'd won.

Clinched a play-off spot. Closed the loop on a brutal start. And they'd done it together.

I leaned against the bench, arms crossed, watching them swarm the ice. Liam tackled Carter. Connor launched his helmet straight up like a firework and nearly brained himself. Ethan? He didn't even celebrate at first. He just stood there, grinning like a man who couldn't believe the finish line was real.

Then he turned—and looked at me.

And everything else blurred.

He skated over slowly, not showing off, no arms flung wide like he used to when he was a kid pretending to win the Stanley Cup in the driveway. This wasn't about show.

This was something else.

Ethan stopped right in front of the bench and looked up at me, eyes bright, face flushed from effort and adrenaline.

"Hell of a season," he said.

I nodded, jaw tight. "You earned it."

He pulled his helmet off—sweaty hair a mess, eyes still locked on mine. "Couldn't have done it without you."

My throat burned.

There was too much in that one line. Everything we hadn't said in years. Everything we'd both nearly lost.

I reached down and pulled him in for a hug, rough and fast, one hand behind his neck, the other clapping hard on his back.

"I'm proud of you," I said, voice barely steady.

"You too, old man," he muttered into my shoulder.

We pulled apart, and he smiled—really smiled.

The team was surging around us now, banging sticks on the boards, dragging me out onto the ice like I hadn't told them twenty times I didn't celebrate like that anymore.

Liam shouted something about lifting me on their shoulders. Carter actually tried.

I swatted them both away, laughing for the first time in what felt like months.

Someone shoved a champagne bottle in my hand.

Connor yelled, "TO COACH VOLKOV—THE HOTTEST SILVER

FOX IN THE LEAGUE."

I shook my head, grinning despite myself, as someone dumped Gatorade on my back and half the staff joined the team dogpile at center ice.

Ethan skated up beside me, raised his bottle, and clinked it against mine.

"To redemption," he said.

I looked at him.

To everything we'd come back from.

To everything we still didn't know how to fix.

To the team that made it matter.

"To redemption," I echoed.

And for the first time in a long time... it felt like maybe we actually had a shot.

Not just at the playoffs.

Not just at repairing something broken.

But at starting again.

43

Chapter 43

Lexi

The air in the locker room was thick with champagne spray and leftover adrenaline. It smelled like victory and sweat and half-eaten pizza—the sweet perfume of a regular season win that meant more than any of us could say out loud.

I sat on a bench beside Connor, his curls still damp from the post-game shower, a towel slung low around his waist like he was born to be interviewed in GQ.

"You're not even gonna ask how I did out there?" he asked, mock-offended, shoving the remnants of a donut in his mouth. "Lex, I assisted that final goal with my mind."

"I saw it," I said, grinning. "Very telekinetic of you."

He pointed at me with half a donut. "Finally. Recognition."

I rolled my eyes and bumped my shoulder into his. "Proud of you, donut boy."

He was still laughing when the locker room door opened.

And Ethan walked in.

Everyone stilled—just for a second. Then Connor, Carter, Liam, the rest of them—they cleared out like a silent command had been issued. No teasing. No jokes.

Just quiet understanding.

I stood slowly, heart thudding as Ethan approached.

His helmet was off, damp hair pushed back, jaw tight like he'd been working himself up to this for hours. His eyes found mine—and stayed there.

"Can we talk?" he asked, voice low. Careful.

I nodded. "Yeah."

The door clicked softly behind the last guy to leave.

Suddenly, the room felt too big. Too empty. Too quiet.

I crossed my arms, tried to stay standing even though my legs felt like warm Jell-O. My stomach knotted. Every part of me braced.

Ethan ran a hand through his hair. "It's been a month."

"I know."

"You've barely looked at me."

"I know that too."

He let out a short breath—a laugh that didn't hold any sharp edges. Just exhaustion. "I deserved it."

I hesitated. Swallowed hard.

"You didn't deserve the silence," I said quietly. "But I didn't know how to come to you. I thought... maybe the best time would be when *you* were ready. Not when I needed it."

He looked up at that. Really looked.

I took a breath that barely stayed inside my chest.

"I'm sorry," I said, voice trembling. "For falling for him. For falling for your dad. It was never supposed to happen—it wasn't planned, and it sure as hell wasn't something I wanted to hurt you with." My throat tightened. "But it happened. And

I've hated myself every day since for not stopping it sooner. For not telling you sooner. For making it harder."

He stepped a little closer, hands tucked in his hoodie pockets, eyes softening.

"I've had a lot of time to think," he said. "About... all of it. About you. And him. And me."

I wiped my hand under my eye. Tried to stay still.

"I've watched my dad show up for me every day for the past month," he said. "He's been steady. Unbelievably patient. Put me first over and over again. Even when I was being an asshole."

"Ethan—"

"Let me finish," he cut in gently, his voice cracking. "I know he hurt me. I know you both did. But I've also seen what it's costing him to stay away from you."

Tears stung the back of my eyes.

"And you..." He exhaled, shaking his head. "You've been walking around like a ghost. Like you left something behind and don't know how to get it back."

"Because I did," I whispered. "I lost you. And I lost him. And I didn't know how to carry both at once."

His expression twisted for a second—like he felt every word.

"I'm not gonna pretend to be okay with it," he said. "Because I'm not. Not fully. Not yet."

I nodded, tears rolling freely now.

"But I'm not gonna stand in the way anymore either."

That cracked something deep inside me.

"I don't want to be the reason either of you are in pain," he said. "I don't want to be what breaks you. Or him."

I pressed a hand to my chest, tried to breathe through it.

"You're not," I said. "You never were. You're the only reason we both tried to do the right thing. And I'm so sorry that it still hurt you."

He swallowed hard, blinking fast.

"And—" he cleared his throat, voice rough. "More than anything... I want my friend back."

That broke me.

Tears spilled over again. I didn't try to stop them.

"I miss you," I said. "So much."

"I miss you too," he said, stepping forward. "You were my best friend before all of this. And I don't want to lose that."

I nodded, my lip trembling.

"I can't promise I'll be totally cool with everything," he added, rubbing the back of his neck. "But I'll try. That's what I've got."

"That's everything," I whispered.

He opened his arms, just slightly. Like he wasn't sure I'd say yes.

I crossed the room and wrapped mine around him before he could blink.

He hugged me back tight—tight enough to feel every word we didn't say.

And for the first time in weeks, the ache in my chest eased just enough to breathe.

44

Chapter 44

Lexi

I stared at the ceiling like it had answers.

It didn't. Obviously. But I was out of other options.

The season was over. The confetti had fallen, the champagne had been popped, and the team was out somewhere celebrating like the world hadn't just tilted off its axis for me.

James hadn't spoken to me.

Not after the game.

Not after Ethan.

Nothing.

And maybe I understood. Maybe I even respected it. But it didn't stop the ache. The slow, gnawing kind that nestled in my chest and whispered *he's really gone* every time I blinked.

I buried myself deeper into the couch, hoodie pulled tight around my knees, like maybe I could curl small enough that the world would forget I existed.

Then, from across the apartment, I heard the rustle of fabric. The unmistakable sound of a closet being ransacked.

Followed by a very specific kind of sigh—Rachel's signature exasperation with a hint of diva flair.

"Lex," she called, stepping into the hallway, hands on her hips, one eyebrow raised so high it could apply for sainthood. "The team ball is tonight."

"I'm aware."

"You were invited."

"Also aware."

"You're not going."

"Correct."

She let out a sigh so full of judgment it should've been framed and mounted. "You're really going to skip the one night where you get to wear something fancy, drink champagne for free, and not be stuck behind a camera like some PR goblin?"

"Yes."

"And this has *nothing* to do with a certain glowering Russian coach who's been walking around like someone murdered his soul?"

"I'm not doing this," I muttered, turning my face into the couch cushion like it might swallow me whole.

Rachel crossed the room and knelt beside me, resting her chin on the armrest with the kind of casual grace that made me want to throw her decorative pillows at her. "I know you're hurting," she said softly. "But you're not the only one. You two are idiots. Beautiful, complicated, tortured idiots. But idiots."

I didn't answer.

I couldn't.

"Talk to me," she whispered.

I pulled the hoodie tighter, voice quiet. "Ethan gave us his blessing."

Rachel blinked. "Wait, what?"

"He pulled me aside. Said he didn't want to stand in the way. Said he saw what it was doing to both of us."

She blinked again, slower this time. "And James still hasn't—?"

I shook my head. "Nothing. Not a text. Not a call. Not even a smoke signal."

Rachel's face fell, just slightly. "Lexi..."

"What if he changed his mind?" My voice cracked. "What if Ethan let us go... and James just didn't want to come back?"

She opened her mouth, but I kept going.

"What if all the reasons he stayed away—Ethan, the timing, the mess—what if now that those are gone, he's realized I wasn't worth the fallout?"

Silence.

Then Rachel climbed up onto the couch beside me and pulled me into her lap like I was five and had scraped my knees on the pavement of life.

"Okay, first of all, fuck that," she said, petting my hair like I was a tragic woodland creature. "Second of all, James Volkov looked at you like you hung the goddamn moon. And third..." She shifted, pulling back just enough to look me in the eye. "He's terrified."

"Of what?"

"Of being happy. Of losing you. Of getting something right for once and not knowing what the hell to do with it."

"So ghosting me was the answer?"

Rachel shrugged. "Men are emotionally constipated, Lex. Sometimes their solution to love is hiding in their metaphorical bat caves and brooding until someone smacks them with a clue-by-four."

I huffed a laugh. "You're terrible at comfort."

"And yet I'm always right."

She stood and brushed her hands off like she'd completed a sacred task. "Now. If you change your mind..."

"About what?"

"The dress in the bathroom."

I blinked. "What dress?"

She smirked. "The one James had delivered three days ago. I hid it because I knew you'd throw it in the trash in a fit of noble heartbreak."

My stomach dropped.

"He what?"

"Yeah." She turned back toward the hall. "Custom label. No return slip. And probably paid for in blood or vodka. So maybe he hasn't said anything—but he said *enough.*"

She paused in the doorway, voice soft now.

"He's not done, Lex. Not even close. And neither are you."

Then she disappeared behind the bathroom door.

And I was left with the silence.

And a dress.

And the tiniest flicker of hope catching fire in the center of my chest.

45

Chapter 45

James

The arena parking lot buzzed with pre-event energy—guys in suits, ties crooked, joking and chirping like they were heading into Game 7, not a formal banquet.

But all I could think about was the one person who wasn't here.

Lexi.

I adjusted the cuffs of my shirt, checking my watch for the fifth time in ten minutes.

She wasn't late.

But she wasn't here either.

I told myself it was fine. That it didn't matter. That I could handle seeing her tonight—or not seeing her. That I'd survived two months of silence, I could survive one more night.

But my gut twisted like I was standing at center ice in the last seconds of a tied game. Because if she didn't show up tonight... I didn't know if I could keep pretending I didn't miss her like hell.

Liam slung an arm over Carter's shoulder as they walked past me toward the coach. "Place your bets, boys. Think Lexi's coming?"

"She better," Carter said, adjusting his collar. "Wouldn't be the same without her."

Connor nodded, already halfway through a Red Bull. "Feels weird without her running around with a camera or threatening to post our worst angles."

"She always makes the ball more fun," Liam said. "It's, like, tradition."

Ethan, hanging back by the doors, chimed in without looking up from his phone. "It'd be sad if she missed it. She's family."

That stopped me cold.

I glanced his way, but he didn't meet my eyes.

Just pocketed his phone and stepped onto the coach with the others.

It hit me then—harder than I expected.

Everyone wanted her there.

Not because she was the social media manager. Not because of me. Just... because she mattered. Because they loved her.

Because she was Lexi.

And I wasn't the only one who felt the gap she left behind.

I turned toward the parking lot, heart thudding, eyes searching for a flash of her car. For anything.

But the spot next to mine was still empty.

And I was starting to wonder if this night was going to break me more than I'd already let it.

* * *

The bus pulled up in front of the hotel just as the sky dipped into early evening, casting a warm gold glow over the red carpet set up outside. Fans had gathered behind velvet ropes, flashing lights already going off before the first pair of polished dress shoes even hit the pavement.

Liam was the first off the coach, grinning like he was walking into the NHL Awards, soaking in every second like it was his natural habitat.

"Try not to look too miserable, Coach," Carter muttered behind me as we stepped off. "You're in a suit. We clean up good."

I adjusted my jacket, exhaled, and followed the team toward the press line.

The cameras clicked like machine guns.

Flash.

Flash.

Flash.

Connor leaned into one of the reporters with a practiced smile. "We're not used to looking this good—don't get used to it."

The crowd laughed. The boys thrived on it. And usually, I could fake it too. Keep the expression sharp, confident. Give them what they wanted.

But my mind wasn't here.

Not really.

I walked down the carpet, blinking through the glare of camera lights, offering nods and handshakes while my ears buzzed with noise.

"Coach Volkov!" a reporter called. "How does it feel leading the team through such an impressive season?"

I paused just long enough to answer.

"Proud of the team," I said automatically. "They've earned

it."

"Only two losses all season—what's been the key to keeping them so consistent?"

"We've built something solid. They trust each other. And they've stayed hungry."

More questions. Player dynamics. Off-ice chemistry. Leadership growth. I answered all of it like I was supposed to.

Then came the shift.

"Coach—about the incident mid-season, with you and Number 91—any comments on that fight?"

I froze for a fraction of a second. Just long enough for the cameras to catch it.

"Nothing that wasn't already handled on the ice," I said, clipped and final.

They pushed.

"And your son—Ethan Wilson—was involved in an altercation just a few weeks later. Unusual for a team with such discipline. Any concerns about emotional leadership?"

My jaw clenched.

"My concern," I said slowly, "is for my players. For the people they are, and the battles they're fighting—on and off the ice. Sometimes, protecting your team means showing them you'll go down swinging."

Pens scratched. Cameras blinked.

Another reporter leaned forward, phone outstretched. "Did you come alone tonight, Coach?"

I paused.

Then gave a single nod.

"Yeah."

A few scribbles. The flash of another camera.

"No date?"

I didn't blink. Just kept my gaze steady. Quiet.

"I came alone," I said, voice low. Measured. "But I wasn't supposed to."

Silence.

I let it settle. Let them lean in.

"I let the wrong thing matter at the worst possible time," I added. "And I lost the only person who ever made me believe I could have something good."

Click. Click. Flash.

They weren't expecting that.

I adjusted my cuff again. Smoothed my lapel.

"Some mistakes," I said, quieter now, "don't hit until it's too late to fix them. And some people... you only meet once."

I didn't wait for more questions.

I stepped off the carpet. Into the hotel.

Alone, still.

But never once—not for a second—without her on my mind.

I stepped away from the press, ignoring the last few questions, and followed the team inside.

Because the night was just beginning—

And already, I couldn't wait for it to be over.

* * *

I barely made it three steps into the lobby before I felt a hand tap my arm.

I turned—and found Ethan standing there in his perfectly tailored black suit, hair slicked back, expression uncharacteristically serious.

"Hey," he said. "Got a sec?"

I nodded and followed him to a quiet corner, away from the cameras, away from the crowd.

For a second, he didn't say anything. Just shifted his weight and glanced toward the carpet where the others were still posing and laughing.

Then he looked at me.

"I just wanted to say... thanks.... again"

My brow furrowed slightly.

Then I said, quietly, "I'd do anything to support you. You know that, right?"

He gave a small nod.

"I'm not going anywhere," I added. "Even when the interim contract's up, I'm going to fight for this job. If it means I get to keep working with you—keep building this thing we started—I'll make it happen. I'll figure out how to run the rest of my businesses from here. I can juggle it."

"You'd stay?" he asked, a little stunned. "Permanently?"

"If it means I get to be in your life? Yeah," I said. "Absolutely."

His expression shifted—something softer, something real.

"I'd like that. Now maybe it's time we get you the girl?"

I blinked.

Swallowed hard.

"Might be too late for that," I said, my voice low.

Ethan tilted his head, watching me carefully. "You really think she's the kind of girl who'd give up that easy?"

I said nothing.

He sighed. Shoved his hands into the pockets of his suit jacket. "You don't get it, do you?"

I glanced at him.

"She loves you, dad." He said it so casually, like it was

obvious. Like it was gravity. "She *hates* how much she loves you—but it's not something she can shut off."

I looked down, jaw clenched. The thought of her—curled on a couch somewhere, avoiding the crowd, still wearing that damn hoodie of mine—made my chest ache.

"She's not here," I muttered.

Ethan gave the smallest smirk. "You really think she'd miss this?"

I raised an eyebrow.

"She'll come," he said confidently, almost like it was a dare to the universe. "Lexi might be dramatic, but she's not a runner. She shows up. Every time. Especially when it's hard."

I looked toward the ballroom entrance. Still no sign of her.

"She's probably standing in front of the mirror right now trying to decide if she's going to kill you or kiss you," he added with a shrug. "Maybe both."

That almost made me laugh.

Almost.

46

Chapter 46

James

The ballroom lights shimmered off crystal chandeliers like stars fallen to earth, and the buzz of conversation rose around me—champagne flutes clinking, polite laughter ricocheting through gold-tinted walls.

But none of it touched me.

I stood alone in the corner of the room, drowning in my own silence. The suit was tight across my shoulders. My collar itched like a noose. And my heart was still somewhere on the locker room floor, cracked open with everything I hadn't let myself say.

Then it happened.

A hush.

One breathless ripple of stillness across the crowd.

And the first haunting notes of **You and Me by Lifehouse** spilled into the air like a secret only the two of us would understand.

I turned.

My eyes swept across the ballroom—and lifted.

And there she was.

Lexi.

At the top of the staircase like a goddess dropped from Olympus to ruin me.

Time didn't just stop. It collapsed.

Her dress was black. Timeless. Liquid shadows clinging to every curve like it knew she'd walked through hell just to stand there. The slit up her leg, the glint of her heels, the fall of her hair over one shoulder—every piece of her carved into my memory before I could even take a full breath.

But it wasn't the dress.

It was her.

Her eyes.

Locked on mine.

Glassy. Wide. Alive with something that undid me.

My hands itched to touch her. My body remembered every place she used to belong. But I didn't move.

Not until she did.

One step.

Measured.

Deliberate.

Like she was choosing.

Like she knew the world might break beneath her heels but she was walking toward me anyway.

The lump in my throat burned like fire. I couldn't swallow. Couldn't breathe.

No one else in the ballroom moved. No one dared.

They could all feel it—that something sacred was about to ignite.

So I moved.

First a step.

Then another.

Then I was running.

Not for the applause. Not for the forgiveness.

For her.

Shouldering through the crowd like gravity was no longer optional. Taking the stairs two at a time because if I didn't reach her, I was going to fucking combust.

"You and me and all of the people, and I don't know why, I can't keep my eyes off of you..."

And then I was there.

Close enough to touch.

Close enough to burn.

But I didn't.

Not yet.

Because she was crying—and smiling—and looking at me like I was something she'd only seen in dreams.

"All of the things that I want to say just aren't coming out right, I'm tripping on words, you've got my head spinning I don't know where to go from here. Cause its you and me..."

"I didn't think you'd come," I said, my voice wrecked and shaking.

"I almost didn't," she breathed.

"Why did you?"

She swallowed. "Because no matter how hard I tried... I couldn't stop needing you."

A single tear slid down her cheek.

And I stepped closer, barely a breath between us. "Lexi," I whispered, "do you remember what I said that night under the stars?"

She nodded once. Fragile. Fierce. "Say it again."

I cupped her face—God, that face—my thumbs brushing away the tears like I had the right.

And I whispered:

"Вы – это момент. Тот, кого хочется помнить, даже когда все остальное уже ушло. Я люблю тебя, котёнок."

You are the moment. The one I want to remember, even when everything else has gone. I love you, kotyonok.

She broke.

Beautifully.

Tears spilling down her cheeks as she leaned into my hands like they were home. Her lips trembled. "I love you too," she whispered. "So much."

And I kissed her.

Not for show.

Not for closure.

But like a man who had waited his whole fucking life to taste the truth.

Slow. Intense. All in.

I kissed her like I was carving a promise into the space between our ribs—*I'm here. I'm yours. I'll never leave again.*

Then I pulled her close.

Dipped her low.

And kissed her again, deeper this time—like a vow.

The room exploded behind us—cheers, whistles, applause.

But all I saw was her.

Just her.

Her hands around my neck.

Her heart against mine.

Her eyes, brighter than anything in that golden ballroom.

And as I brought her back upright, as she laughed through tears, as the last words of the song wrapped around us like silk—

"And I don't know why, I can't take my eyes off of you..."

—I knew.

This was the moment.

The one they'd talk about for years.

The one they'd whisper about in corners and replay on shaky phone videos.

The one that rewrote everything.

Because this wasn't scandal.

This wasn't chaos.

This was *love*.

Real. Raw. Relentless.

And this time?

We weren't hiding it anymore.

I didn't let her go.

Not even when the applause roared around us like a standing ovation for something we hadn't planned—only survived.

I kept my arms around her waist, holding her tight against me, forehead pressed to hers. Her breath fanned across my lips, still uneven, still trembling. I felt her hands curl into the lapels of my suit like she didn't quite trust the ground beneath her feet.

Neither did I.

"It's really you," I whispered.

She gave a tiny laugh, choked and full of disbelief. "It's really me."

We stayed like that—just us, breathing each other in while the world slowly faded back into motion around us. The music drifted into the next track, something low and romantic, but I barely registered it. She was the only rhythm I cared about.

"You look..." I shook my head, stunned all over again. "I don't even have the words."

Her smile tilted. "Try."

"Unreal," I said. "Like the version of you I see when I close my eyes and wish I could go back."

Her expression softened, eyes glassy. "You're really not going anywhere this time?"

I shook my head. "Not if you'll have me."

She leaned into me, arms wrapping around my neck, and pressed her cheek to mine. "I'll always have you. I never stopped needing you."

I closed my eyes and breathed her in.

Vanilla. Citrus. Home.

There was something about holding her in front of everyone—no more secrets, no more hiding—that loosened a knot in my chest I didn't know I was still carrying. This wasn't just a kiss. This was us finally *choosing* each other. Out loud. Without apology.

"They're all still staring," she murmured after a moment, and I could feel the smile on her lips.

"Let them," I said, not pulling back. "They've stared at worse."

She laughed again, and God, I missed that sound. That bright, reckless laugh that made everything feel lighter.

"You know," I said, brushing a lock of hair from her cheek, "I think I'm in real danger of never letting you out of my sight again."

She tilted her head, all teasing eyes. "That doesn't sound so dangerous."

"It is," I said, my voice low as I leaned in again, kissing her slowly, deeply—less fireworks this time and more gravity. The kind that anchors you. The kind that stays.

When we finally broke apart again, the crowd had moved on—mostly. The boys were back to drinking and joking, Rachel was squealing somewhere across the room, and the lights had dimmed for dinner.

But she stayed in my arms.

And for the first time in months, I didn't feel like I was pretending.

I just felt like hers.

47

Chapter 47

Lexi

My hand was still wrapped in his.

Warm. Sure. Steady.

And I was still trying to believe this was real.

The music, the kiss, the applause—all of it felt like something out of a dream I'd never dared to let myself finish. But now... now he was beside me again. No hiding. No fear. Just him. Just me.

Us.

We stood at the top of the staircase for a moment longer, our breathing finally slowing, our fingers still laced together like we didn't quite trust what might happen if we let go.

"You ready?" he asked, quietly, leaning close.

I looked down at the glittering ballroom below—our teammates, the management, the press, the swirl of champagne and music and celebration. People we loved. People who'd watched us fall apart. And now? They were watching something new begin.

I nodded. "Yeah. Let's go."

James kept hold of my hand as we descended the steps together. I was hyper-aware of every eye on us, every camera lens subtly angled in our direction, but for once, it didn't bother me. I didn't feel like a story waiting to be written.

I felt like I was finally living the ending *I* chose.

"Damn," Carter said as we reached the floor, giving us a low whistle. "That entrance was Oscar-worthy."

Connor grinned. "You two just blew up social media. I can *feel* it."

"Seriously," Liam added, raising his glass. "About time you idiots figured your shit out."

I laughed, heart fluttering with something I hadn't felt in weeks—joy. "I missed you guys."

"Missed *you*, Lex," Connor said, pulling me into a quick hug. "You've been a ghost lately. And not the fun, haunting-people kind."

Rachel appeared at my side like she'd materialized from thin air, eyes wide and sparkling. "Girl. You *dipped.* At the top of the stairs. In a dress with a slit. In heels. And didn't fall."

"She nailed it," James said, smirking as he slid his arm around my waist. "I just got lucky enough to be there for it."

Rachel wiggled her brows at me. "We're going to unpack *everything* later."

I smiled at her, and for the first time in months, it wasn't forced.

The rest of the evening blurred into soft laughter, flickering candlelight, stolen glances, and quiet brushes of his fingers against mine under the table. The music pulsed, the speeches were made, the glasses clinked.

But all I could feel was him.

* * *

The laughter and clinking glasses faded into the background as the band shifted gears, the lights dimming to a warm golden hue that spilled across the ballroom like honey.

Then—just guitar strings.

Soft. Simple. Familiar.

The acoustic version of *"Beautiful Crazy"* **by Luke Combs** floated through the speakers, and I swear my heart stopped.

James was already watching me.

He stood slowly, his gaze never leaving mine, and extended a hand across the table.

"Dance with me," he said, voice low and gentle, like he knew the answer but still needed to ask.

I barely nodded before slipping my fingers into his. The moment I touched him, everything else in the ballroom seemed to blur. The music, the people, the flicker of candlelight—it all fell away.

He led me to the dance floor.

And pulled me into him.

His hand slid around my waist, the other lacing with mine. I rested my free hand against his chest, over the steady thud of his heart, and let him sway me into the rhythm of the song.

"When she gets that come-get-me look in her eyes. Well, it kinda scares me, the way that she drives me wild...."

"I think this might be my favourite song now," I whispered against his collar.

He smiled, a little sad, a little in awe. "I was thinking the same thing."

We danced like no one was watching—though I could feel every eye in the room. But they didn't matter. Not when I was pressed this close to him. Not when I could feel his breath in my hair, his thumb brushing soft, absent minded circles against the small of my back.

"I used to dream about this," I murmured. "You. Me. Dancing in front of everyone but still feeling like it's just us."

"You still dreaming now?" he asked.

I looked up at him. "Not anymore."

We kept moving, slow and quiet, as Luke's voice echoed through the room like it had been written just for us.

"Beautiful, crazy... she can't help but amaze me..."

He leaned down, his forehead gently pressing to mine.

"I don't care who's watching," he murmured. "You look like everything I've ever wanted."

I smiled, heart thudding painfully in my chest. "You don't look so bad yourself, Volkov."

His grip tightened just slightly. "You make me feel twenty again."

"You make me feel like I'm not going to break anymore."

He didn't answer. Just kissed me.

Softly.

Right there, in the middle of the dance floor.

The kind of kiss that didn't need an audience.

The kind that said everything we'd never been brave enough to say out loud.

And as the song reached its final note, fading into the hum of the ballroom again, he leaned close and whispered in Russian—

"Ты мой конец и моё начало. Мой грех. Моё спасение. Моя любовь."

You are my end and my beginning. My sin. My salvation. My love.

And I felt it—deep in my bones.

This wasn't a reunion.

This was home.

* * *

The song faded, but we didn't move.

He kept holding me like we had all the time in the world, and for once, I let myself believe that maybe we did.

The lights brightened slightly, the dance floor slowly repopulated with couples. Someone popped a bottle of champagne. Laughter returned. Life moved on.

But we stayed in our little pocket of peace, his arms around me, my heart finally steady.

Then he leaned down, brushing his lips to my temple.

"You wanna get out of here?" he asked, voice quiet but full of something warm and wicked.

I pulled back just enough to look up at him. "What, tired of being the most romantic man in the room?"

His smile curved—slow, private. "Not tired. Just ready for something better."

I arched a brow. "Better than this?"

He dipped his head to whisper in my ear. "I reserved the penthouse suite."

I blinked. "You did *what*?"

He stepped back just enough to let me see the glint in his eyes. "Penthouse. Top floor. Private balcony. Firelight. Silk

262

sheets."

I stared at him, stunned. "You reserved that for tonight?"

His gaze held mine.

Then he said it.

Voice low. Serious. Certain.

"Baby... I bought this whole hotel for you."

I blinked. "You—what?"

"I bought it when they announced the event was being hosted here. Just in case you came. Just in case I needed that room."

My mouth fell open.

"You *bought the hotel*," I repeated.

"Yes."

My heart. Literally. Stopped.

And then I laughed, breathless and completely undone. "That's... insane."

He leaned in, brushing a kiss just below my ear. "So is the way I love you."

And with that, he took my hand.

And I followed him.

48

Chapter 48

Lexi

The elevator doors slid closed with a soft chime.

The second we were alone, everything shifted.

James hit the button for the top floor, then turned toward me—eyes dark, jaw tight, chest rising and falling like he'd been holding back for hours.

"I've waited too long for this," he growled.

Then he was on me.

His mouth crashed into mine, hot and wild, no patience left. His hands roamed fast, possessive—one gripping my waist, the other sliding up my spine like he needed to remind himself I was real. I gasped into his kiss, my back hitting the wall of the elevator with a soft thud.

His mouth dropped to my neck, teeth grazing skin as his hand slipped under the slit of my gown, up my thigh, fingers dragging over bare skin like he was starved for it. The elevator hummed beneath us, the floor numbers blinking past one by one.

"I've spent months trying to forget this," he whispered against my skin. "Trying to erase the way you feel under me. The way you sound when you fall apart in my arms. I couldn't. I *can't*."

I whimpered, already unraveling, already burning for him.

The elevator doors slid closed, and before I could take a breath, James had me pinned.

His mouth crashed into mine, hands already everywhere—tugging at the slit of my dress, gripping my thigh, dragging me closer like he was afraid I'd vanish if he didn't get to me fast enough.

"James—"

"No," he rasped. "Not tonight. Just *feel me*, kotyonok."

The elevator dinged. He didn't let go. Just smirked against my lips, adjusted his jacket like he hadn't just made me come undone with a kiss, and guided me down the hall like a man on a mission.

The penthouse was warm and golden, the flicker of firelight dancing over polished floors. City lights glittered beyond the glass like they were watching us, waiting for the inevitable.

He turned to face me, eyes dark.

"Shoes. Off. Now."

I obeyed, heart pounding.

He stalked toward me, slowly, deliberately, and spun me around, the zipper of my dress slipping down with a quiet hiss.

"Lie down," he murmured. "I need to taste you."

I barely hit the bed before he was between my thighs, spreading me open like a man starving. His mouth was everywhere—hot, wet, unrelenting. Tongue flicking, licking, sucking until I was gasping, writhing, pulling at his hair with shaking hands.

When he slid two fingers inside me and curled just right, I

shattered, crying out his name.

But he wasn't done.

He kissed up my body, slow and reverent, and hovered over me, eyes blown wide with hunger.

"Tell me you're mine."

"I'm yours," I whispered. "Always."

He thrust into me in one powerful stroke, groaning like he was finally home.

It was raw. Desperate. His hands tangled in my hair as his hips pounded into mine. He kissed me like he needed it to breathe, muttering dirty Russian against my skin, every word making me wetter, needier, more unhinged.

"Ты моя," he growled. *You're mine.*

And God—I was.

Before I could catch my breath, he flipped me, dragging me toward the glass windows.

"Hands on the glass," he ordered. "I want the whole damn city to see how I fuck you."

I braced myself, breath fogging the glass as he drove into me from behind, one hand tangled in my hair, the other gripping my hip like he'd never let go. The view blurred as my eyes rolled back—his voice in my ear, his body pounding into mine, the filthy things he said making me fall apart all over again.

He came with a deep groan, collapsing against my back, his breath hot on my neck.

But he wasn't done.

He carried me to the bathroom, setting me gently into the hot, steaming tub. Then he sank into the water with me, pulling me into his lap.

Slow this time.

Intimate.

I wrapped my arms around his neck, sinking down onto him with a gasp as his hands slid over my slick, wet skin like he couldn't get enough of touching me.

"Look at me," he whispered. "I want to see you when you come."

I moved over him slowly, our bodies perfectly in sync, my moans echoing off the tile, his name the only word I could say. He kissed me over and over, like he was imprinting this moment onto my soul.

And when we both broke again, limbs tangled, hearts racing—

He didn't let go.

He held me there.

Safe.

Wrecked.

His.

49

Chapter 49

✧ *Epilogue – One Year Later*

Part 1: Lexi

The same hotel. The same ballroom. The same glittering chandeliers and overpriced champagne.

But everything felt different.

I stood at the top of the grand staircase again, only this time, there was no fear in my chest. No weight in my throat. Just a simple, grounding warmth as I looked out over the crowd below.

Because this time—I wasn't wondering if he'd be there.

He was already waiting for me.

James looked up the second I stepped into view, and the second our eyes met, that same electric pull hit me. Only now, it wasn't dangerous. It was home.

His smile was soft, barely visible to anyone else, but I saw it.

Because I always did.

He met me at the bottom of the stairs and pulled me in with one hand on my waist, the other settling on my cheek.

Which, honestly—it kind of did.

"Hi, kotyonok," he whispered.

"Hi."

His lips brushed my temple as the band started a familiar tune—*Beautiful Crazy*, acoustic, again. My heart flipped.

"You really requested it again?" I teased.

"You wore the same dress," he murmured, "it just seemed right."

I laughed, then looked down as his thumb grazed the tiny bump under the soft satin of my gown. Barely there. But real.

"Can you believe this time last year we were still sneaking around?"

He smile, a real and genuine smile. "I can't quite believe you've been mine for a whole year."

We danced, slowly, the world fading around us again. Somewhere nearby, Rachel was probably holding court, and Connor was definitely making a scene. But none of it touched this little bubble around us.

Just like last time.

Only now... everything was out in the open.

My ring caught the light as James twirled me once, then pulled me back in, his forehead pressing to mine.

"I'm so glad you came back that night," he whispered.

"I never really left you," I said.

His hand cupped my cheek, eyes burning. "Marry me sooner."

"James."

"I'm serious."

"You've already got me."

269

"I want all of you. Forever."

I kissed him before I could say anything else.

And it didn't matter that we were in front of everyone.

Because this was ours.

And always would be.

50

Chapter 50

Part 2: Ethan

I leaned against the edge of the bar, sipping something sparkling I wasn't in the mood for, watching the dance floor with a strange ache in my chest.

But not the bad kind.

Not anymore.

They looked... right.

James and Lexi.

Laughing. Spinning. Him holding her like he couldn't believe she was real. Her glowing like she'd finally stopped pretending she was fine.

They didn't see anyone else.

And I guess that was the point.

"You okay?" Rachel's voice broke through beside me, gentle and knowing.

I nodded. "Yeah. Actually, I am."

She followed my gaze, her own smile soft. "They're kinda perfect, huh?"

I let out a quiet breath. "Yeah. They are."

It took me a long time to admit that.

Even longer to stop being angry.

But watching them now... the way she leaned into him, the way he held her like she was the only thing that ever mattered— I finally understood.

It was never about betrayal.

It was about love.

And if there's one thing I've learned over the last year?

Love doesn't ask permission.

It doesn't care about timing or logic or rules. It just happens—loud and messy and real.

I watched them dance until the song faded, until the lights shifted, until it wasn't their moment anymore.

And for once... I didn't wish it was mine.

Not because I didn't love her once.

But because I finally understood what it meant to let go.

Some love stories aren't meant to be chapters.

They're just the prologue to your own.

And maybe—just maybe—mine was still out there, waiting to be written.

Afterword

If you made it to the end of *Power Play*—first of all, thank you. Second of all... are you okay? Do you need ice? A hug? A therapist who specializes in fictional men with emotional repression issues?

Lexi and James were never supposed to happen. But then again, the best stories usually start with "this is a terrible idea."

This book was for the ones who've sworn off love, only to have it crash into their life in the form of a broody, rule-breaking ex-player with a tragic past and a talent for making bad decisions feel *so good*.

If you laughed, cried, yelled at Lexi through your screen, or found yourself daydreaming about being pinned against your desk by a man in a suit—thank you for reading. Truly.

And if you're the type of reader who *loves* messy men with redemption arcs?

Good. Because Ethan Wilson is next.

He's got a chip on his shoulder, a reputation to outrun, and one very big problem:

His best friend's little sister just walked back into his life.

All grown up.

All off-limits.

And absolutely determined to ruin his plans.

Book Two is coming. It's hot. It's angsty. It's morally questionable.
You've been warned.

With love and chaos,
Jade

Book Two Teaser

Penalty Box - COMING SOOON

He's trying to stay out of trouble. She *is* the trouble.

"He's done playing games. Until her."

Want a little teaser for book 2...

Some rules were never meant to be broken.
Like don't touch your best friend's sister.
Especially when he's the golden boy of hockey—
And you're the cautionary tale who blew it all up.
He knows what it means to screw up.
To lose everything.
To hurt someone you promised to protect.
Now he's trying to clean up the wreckage.
Rebuild what's left of his name.
Prove that he's not that guy anymore.
But then she walks back into his life.
His best friend's little sister.
The girl he used to pretend not to notice—
Now fully grown, sharp-tongued, and absolutely off-limits.
He's trying to be better.
But she's everything he shouldn't want...

And the only thing that makes him feel like he might still be worth saving.
Because redemption doesn't come easy.
And the heart doesn't play fair.

Acknowledgements

To everyone who picked up this book and dove into this story—thank you. Whether you laughed, blushed, gasped, or yelled into a pillow... I'm glad you came along for the ride. To the readers who live for slow burns, emotionally complicated men, and heroines who refuse to apologize for being bold—you're my people.

To my friends, thank you for enduring the unhinged voice notes, the mid-draft meltdowns, and the 3 a.m. texts like *"What if the dad is also the coach?"* You never judged me. At least not out loud.

To my husband Luke—thank you for your patience, your love, and for never once asking why the fictional men in my brain get so much attention. Your support means everything. You are the reason I get to chase this dream.

To my beautiful children—you are my light, my laughter, and my greatest inspiration. I hope you grow up knowing you can build anything from passion and persistence. To my family—thank you for being my biggest fans, my loudest supporters, and the first people I run to when I need to be reminded that I can do this. Your belief in me made every page possible.

And finally—to every reader who saw themselves in Lexi's strength, James's struggle, or Ethan's growth: this one was for you. For the ones who pretend they want soft love, but secretly crave the kind that leaves marks. The ones who want to be ruined, not just touched.

We made it.
Now exhale.
Book Two is waiting.
And it's even more unhinged.

About the Author

Jade Charlotte writes messy, magnetic romance for readers who want to scream, cry, and blush—all within the same chapter.

Her stories are built around flawed, impulsive women and the broody, morally questionable men who can't stay away from them. If it's forbidden, complicated, or guaranteed to leave emotional shrapnel? She's writing it.

Power Play is her debut novel, born from a deeply unhealthy obsession with slow-burn tension, power dynamics, and characters who heal each other by breaking every rule along the way.

When she's not writing, she's probably building dramatic playlists that could soundtrack your next poor life decision, whispering plot ideas to her notes app at 3 a.m., or telling herself she's going to "just reread one chapter" and then devouring an entire book in one sitting.

She believes the best love stories are a little bit dangerous. And that every emotionally repressed love interest deserves at least one chance to beg for forgiveness with his whole chest.

Follow her online for sneak peeks, exclusive chaos, and dangerously hot men who ruin everything (in a good way):

Find her on Instagram & Tiktok
📱 @j.adecharlotte